Also by Lady Alexa

A Sissy Cuckold Husband
Sissy Husband 3

Becoming Joanne
Becoming Joanne 1
Becoming Joanne 2
Becoming Joanne 3

Femboy Love
Femboy Love 1

Feminized and Pretty
Feminized and Pretty 1
Feminized and Pretty 3
Feminized and Pretty 4

Forced Feminization

Forced Feminization Bundle 1

Lockdown Feminization
Lockdown Feminization 3
Lockdown Feminization 1

Sissy femboy transgender husband
SIssy Husband 1

Sissy Princess
Sissy Princess 2
Sissy Princess 1

Stepmother's Sissy
Stepmother's Sissy
Stepmother's Sissy 2
Stepmother's Sissy 3

Standalone
A Very Dominant Woman
Sissy Pink

SISSY HUSBAND
3
A cuckold sissy and a strict wife
Lady Alexa

. . ⧉ . .

Lady Alexa Publications

This novel is a work of fiction. Names, characters, businesses, places, events and incidents are either the products of the author's imagination or used in a fictitious manner. Any resemblance to actual persons, living or dead, or actual events is purely coincidental.

This novel contains explicit scenes of a sexual nature including forced male to female gender transformation, female domination, humiliation, CFNM, BDSM, spanking and reluctant feminisation. All characters in this story are aged 18 and over.

Strictly for adults aged 18 and over or the age of maturity in your country.

*Follow me at Amazon by clicking on
https://www.amazon.com/stores/Lady-Alexa/author/
B01HWRGJGW
and then clicking on the follow button to get all my latest
book news.*

*Subscribe to my blog charting my real-life FLR and forced
feminisation lifestyle with my feminised husband Alice here:
www.ladyalexauk.com[1]*

*You can also subscribe to my newsletter from my blog by
clicking on the side bar and entering your email:
<u>www.ladyalexauk.com</u>*

---

1. *http://www.ladyalexauk.com/*

CONTENTS

Sissy Husband 3 is the third book of an updated re-telling of an earlier series called *A Sissy Cuckold Husband* which is now no longer available. The original was a forced feminisation and sissification story where a husband is feminised by a Mistress and his wife as a double act. They turn him into a submissive and cuckolded sissy.

I revisit my older books from time to time to update the covers and some of the inner text. While updating my *A Sissy Cuckold Husband* series, I noticed there was an alternative storyline within the plot – that of husband who visits professional mistresses to live out his sissy fantasy but keeps his femboy dreams a secret from his wife Gemma.

Once Gemma finds out her husband's desires to be a femboy sissy through his former girlfriend, Gemma and her new friend set about realising his and their dream. Her husband Paul pushes back as he tackles his inner societal programming that being a sissy femboy is somehow shameful despite his internal feelings.

The series now has more of a transgender awakening theme and of a mutually agreed relationship that satisfies everyone but is very different to what society considers the norm.

After experiencing the wonders of femdom and forced feminisation, Gemma becomes bored with her vanilla marriage.

When she catches her husband spying on her, she re-starts his sissification and her female domination in their marriage. But it's still not enough. In book 3, she decides to drive her husband deeper into becoming her submissive sissy than before while searching for a real man.

The thing is, she knows that despite his complaints, her husband used to pay mistresses to play at being sissy. Well now, he can be her sissy called Pansy.

Chapter 1: The Voyeur

Gemma Paige loved the way her firm 36DD breasts swayed and bounced inside her sports bra.

She gyrated to the electronic beat blasting from the music system. The floorboards vibrated in her basement home gym and the door rattled in its frame. The louder the music, the better for her. Their house was large and detached; the neighbours would hear nothing from her basement training room. This was her private world and it was loud and fun.

She swivelled her flat bare stomach to the hollered chants and whoops of the video teacher. She wiggled her rounded but firm bottom; she was in her favourite place. Her figure-hugging booty shorts were like a second skin. Her thin black shorts cut into her vagina lips, moulding over her labia like two rich luscious tubes. She enjoyed the feeling of the seam rubbing against her clitoris as she danced. Her dampness was not just sweat from the intense exercise.

Gemma belonged to the most exclusive gym in the city. It was inconvenient to drive there every day and today was one of those days. Besides, her husband, Paul, was coming home early and she wanted to be there for him. She felt horny, despite their intense love-making session before he went to work that morning. She always felt horny after they made love. His tiny dick didn't satisfy her. But love was more than physical, wasn't it? Besides, she had a large rechargeable life-like dildo for when her husband was gone to satisfy her.

She had made him late, sucking on his small erection, licking and blowing it. She laughed to herself, it was like sucking on a real clitoris it was so small. She knew all about sucking on real clitorises. Paul didn't know that little fact. If he'd had his secrets seeing professional mistresses, she could have her secrets about what she'd done with Mistress Karlene. Maybe she'd been a little hasty in kicking her out but things had got out of control and Karlene had become arrogant. Thinking about their private sessions together made her even hotter though. Maybe she could find someone less assertive in the future for that secret fun.

Before Paul had orgasmed that morning, she had sat on top of him, her hips swirling onto his hard tiny penis. Up and down, side to side she had swirled, twisting her body against his hard organ, trying to find some feeling. But it was too small. She had tried rubbing her clitoris against his pubic area for stimulation but he came inside a minute. Again. It was fortunate she loved him but it was frustrating. Once he'd left the house for work, she got out her hidden ten-inch electric dildo and found the satisfaction he couldn't give her. And she'd imagined being with Karlene and Frank, her boyfriend for one night. But what a cock he had. She missed that.

She loved Paul like nothing else, the problem was his tiny three-inch penis left her feeling unsatisfied. He often wept after sex. She was never sure if that was because of the consummation of their love or because of his lack of size down below knowing it left his wife wanting more. Probably both.

He'd also let himself go since the 'Karlene Incident' when they'd turned him into a submissive cuckolded sissy femboy. He knew he was not as masculine as he'd pretended; he was short and with a tiny dick. But she loved him, probably because he was like that. It was a challenge sometimes but you can't have everything. And he was rich which was a huge compensation.

But since the Karlene Incident, Paul had been far more attentive and submissive towards her. Nothing was too much trouble. She had enjoyed it when he was Pansy though and missed those times.

Gemma took a swig of water from her BPA-free sports bottle during a thirty-second break. The video teacher screamed an instruction, the music wound up and she was off again. Now she was in her thirties, she didn't get much work as a supermodel. That didn't mean she had to give up on her appearance. That was a matter of pride.

She bent on all fours, legs and arms straight, backside towards the gym door. Through her legs, she noticed the door was open. She'd closed it when she came in. One half of her husband's face peeked round and a set of fingers held the door a few inches ajar.

She pretended not to see him. It was unusual he hadn't come in to say hello. She wondered how long he had been watching her. She guessed he had been watching her exercise and became excited. She liked to see his desire for her. After three years together, it was wonderful he remained so attracted to her.

Paul was infatuated and that was nice, it meant she had a high level of control in their relationship. All women liked and used their feminine wiles this way. That said, he should have come in and she would have been happy to perform the aerobics routine for him. He didn't need to skulk behind the door in secret. Something was going on.

The music beat quickened and she wiggled her bum in time. Her boobs joined in, moving in synchronisation. She got up, closed her eyes and turned towards her husband, pretending she didn't know he was there. She'd give him something to think about. And find out what he was up to skulking behind the door.

She moved her hands over her breasts, kneading into them slowly and seductively. She swayed her hips one way and the other, tossing her wavy blond hair back from her face. She ran her hands down to her belly, long red nails scratching into her light skin. She pushed her hand down over her booty shorts and onto her large outlined labia. She traced their shape against the taut silky material and pushed a finger in. If Paul wanted a show, he'd love this one.

The door clicked shut. That was odd. She stopped dancing, the music chugged on. She marched to the door and tugged it wide open.

Paul was bent over. He was still in his business suit, his hand rubbing fast at his groin area. His long brown hair fell over his face; he hadn't seen her. He had always worn it long and she made sure it was longer since the Karlene Incident. Karlene had been an overbearing pain but Karlene had known about Paul's submissive sissiness that she hadn't spotted. She liked his feminine side. Or more accurately, his sissy femboy side.

Gemma pulled him up by his shoulder. His tiny erect penis poked out from his flies and his thumb and forefinger held his little retracted foreskin. His eyes blazed wide in horror.

"Were you playing with yourself, Paulie?" She moved in close and looked down on him, four inches taller even in flat sports shoes. "Wasn't our hot love-making enough for you this morning? You want more? You want to spy on your wife?"

His cheeks and neck flushed red and he looked to the floor. He spluttered, unable to articulate a word.

Gemma tingled from the friction on her clitoris from the exercise and the tight shorts. She pushed his chin up with one long slim finger. "It's wonderful I excite you, I suppose." She took his hand and looked at his erection, small and hard. "Something looks pleased to see me. I suppose I should be happy you're whacking off to me rather than for those professional mistresses you used to pay for." An anger built in her at that memory and of him masturbating in secret. He was still being secretive. She couldn't trust him.

His large brown eyes drooped in humiliation. "I'm so sorry Gemma. I saw you in your tight sports clothes and your bottom and breasts looked so sexy. I couldn't help myself. I was only thinking of you"

She put the end of a forefinger under the head of his penis. She lifted it an inch and held it between her thumb and forefinger. Something was stirring inside her, something stimulating, arousing. She wasn't sure if it was the feeling of her breasts, her shorts against her clitoris or the sexual power she had over her husband.

"But you didn't need to hide, did you, Paulie?" She rubbed his foreskin over the end, back and forth, slow and gentle. This sexual power she had over her husband made her feel strong and alive. Why had she stopped her dominance and returned to a vanilla lifestyle?

Paul's breathing increased, louder, deeper as she rubbed his tiny penis. He screwed his face up and closed his eyes tight.

"You like that." Her voice was soft and dreamy. "Pansy." She couldn't help it but she was angry although she hid it well.

His eyes shot open. It was as if he had received an electric shock.

"Gemma?" His voice was low and husky. His eyes were half-closed, seduced by her gentle fingers as they ran over his sensitive penis skin. His large brown eyes drooped. "Please let's not go back to that pansy nonsense again. I thought we'd left that behind us and moved on. It's over. We agreed."

"But you were such a cute sissy, don't you remember?" Gemma shoved her hand inside his trouser fly and held his balls. They were small like little walnuts. She tightened her grip, her lips touched hard against his and she flicked her tongue into his mouth. Her whole body felt stimulated and adrenaline-charged by her visceral feelings at the idea of feminising, sissifying and subduing her small husband once again. She should never have stopped.

"Over, you say?" Her nails dug deeper into the soft skin of his testicles. "That was the just beginning, not the end. A taster. I threw Karlene out as she got too big for her boots. But I loved having a submissive sissy husband. I want that."

She gripped his balls harder with a vice-like hold. He squealed a high-pitched wail that tailed away.

"I like that sound, Pansy Princess. I've missed it."

His secret watching of her dance routine and secret masturbation had reminded her of his desire to be a sissy and awoken the dominance in her. She bent down and kissed him lightly on the lips and moved in so her body pressed against his. Their bodies intertwined, lips locking tighter. She placed her hand on the back of his neck and pulled him in closer. She searched around his ball sacks with the other hand, probing for the small delicate nuggets inside them. Two fragile little almonds. She found them, pecked the end of his nose with soft large lips, smiled sweetly and squeezed for a few moments.

She froze for an instant. "What are you doing?" he panted, tears in his eyes. "That hurt."

She leaned down and kissed around his ears, her hand maintaining the pressure on his nuts. "You were such a cute little femboy when we made you into Pansy." Her voice was rich and sensual, loving and caring. She twisted his balls one way and then the other. His eyes watered and his face winced. She kept his balls clamped hard, her smile bathed her sultry face.

"Let's go upstairs, Pansy Princess, and do what is necessary," she said.

She pulled him towards the stairs by his balls, up to the ground floor, her hand inside his trouser fly clamped tight. He staggered behind her, pulled along by her long slim arm, his face twisted, his eyes wet and pleading. "Gemma, please."

"I want to play." She looked back at her husband. "And you started it by jerking off behind the door, Pansy."

Chapter 2: Memories

Gemma guided her husband up the stairs and along the landing towards the master bedroom. She looked back at him lovingly. He shuffled behind her. He wanted sex with his hot wife and she knew it. He was putty.

She stopped outside their bedroom door and looked down the passage. There was a door at the end. It was shut. Behind the door was the single bedroom that had been her husband's for a couple of days last month. A bedroom decorated like a teenage girl's: pink with posters of naked young men and cartoon princesses on the walls.

Those days seemed like a distant dream. The bedroom was the last reminder of that time. She had become friends with Karlene Adair, the stunning professional dominatrix. They had turned Paul into a little pansy girl. It was no dream. Gemma shivered with the memories. Her round smooth face flushed with warmth and her blue eyes widened. A familiar tingle zinged in her stomach and down to her clitoris.

Gemma sighed at those hot exhilarating memories. Why had she left them behind so suddenly? OK, she'd become annoyed at Karlene's arrogance but maybe she had acted too rashly. She looked back at her husband. His eyes were on the door at the end of the passage too. It was obvious he remembered those days with less enthusiasm. He became his wife's sissy princess with different emotions. His wife had cuckolded him with the tall well-hung beefy Frank. Gemma and Karlene had dressed him as a sissy femboy and forced him to watch as Frank banged his wife with his massive cock.

That had hurt Paul's pride, masculinity and self-worth. Paul closed his eyes and a tear seeped out from one corner and onto the bridge of his nose. The memories hit him hard although there had been something about seeing his wife taken by a real man. Something he couldn't explain that excited him.

Gemma watched him for a moment, the feelings burning again inside her. She had to answer the call. She had tried to return to the normality of a vanilla life with the man she loved but it was proving impossible. The episode in her gym showed that. Her husband's little penis failed to satisfy the urging she had for a real cock to fill her up. She had tasted Frank's eleven inches and it was not possible to return to Paul's pathetic little three inches. It didn't match up in any way. Paul had a clitty, a little *Miss Clitty*. Karlene had ignited something in her and she had to have Pansy Princess to pay with again. This time, she would not give it up.

Gemma guided Paul into the master bedroom. She removed her hand from his flies and pushed the door shut. He tried to put his little erection back into his open trousers. She slapped his hand away and smiled sweetly.

"Wait for me outside the en-suite shower-room door, Princess, I'm going to shower and change."

"Gemma," he said. "Please. I don't want to do the sissy thing again. We left that behind, we made a mistake. Didn't we?" Something in his eyes told Gemma he wasn't being entirely truthful.

Gemma moved in close to him, she pushed her body into his tiny erection. She rubbed her fingertips on his cheek. "Pansy darling, you're such a sweetie." She pressed her lips against his. "Be a good sissy boy and wait by the door until I'm ready." She brushed the hair away from his face. She was pleased she made him keep his hair long. Why had she done that? Had she always meant to return to this?

"This is ridiculous." He pouted.

She moved down and kissed him on his nose and a smile grew on her wide luscious lips. She ran her tongue along his lips, first the top then along the bottom. A mischievous sultry glint sparkled in her eyes. He closed his eyes, taking in her affection. Her hand went to his erection and slid inside and wrapped around his balls. She touched them with her smooth gentle fingertips. He moaned in pleasure. She fondled his balls. He hummed a deep sound and closed his eyes. She squeezed short and hard and he squealed.

Gemma whispered in his ear. "Pansy-boy, when I tell you to do something, you do it." She kissed his ear, tucked his hair behind it and continued stroking his head.

"Yes, yes. OK. Please stop, Gemma, it hurts. You'll damage them."

"You're an adorable little girly femboy when you do what your Goddess tells you. But punishment will be swift when you don't. It's your choice, sissy." Gemma pulled her hand away and Paul let out a deep breath. "Wait here and don't touch Miss Clitty, you know I don't like that. But leave it poking out of your flies as it looks cute that way. You should display her for me more often, baby."

Gemma strode to the en-suite bathroom, leaving the door open. She pulled off her sports bra and her firm boobs bounced clear. She dropped the bra on the floor. She bent down and rolled off her booty shorts. She kicked them away. Paul stared back at her, desire burned in his face and his eyes flowed over his wife's naked body. They had been married for three years, but she knew he never got bored with her incredible figure. His erection showed her that.

She was 5ft 10inches of slim, lean elegant muscle and smooth clear skin. She had a small waist, wide hips and a pert round bum. She let him feast his eyes on her 36DD breasts, firm and voluptuous. She smiled at him, a generous kind look. "You know I adore you, Pansy."

She watched as he looked over her hips and down to her pubic area. A thin Brazilian line of blond pubic hair led to her swollen labia; her erect clitoris protruded slightly. Paul panted. She knew he had secretly enjoyed being a pansy when Karlene had been there. He would never admit it but she had seen his demeanour during that time with Karlene and her lover, Frank. Her husband's near-permanent erection during that time told her everything she needed to know about Pansy's desires. Feminisation and cuckolding were deep desires she intended to re-instigate.

Gemma stepped into the double-length glass shower cubicle and flipped on the jet of water. She lathered her body with a fresh bar of creamy soap. She rubbed her calves and up to her thighs. Paul's eyes locked onto Gemma. He followed her soapy hands as they edged closer to her vagina lips. His mouth opened and his tongue lolled. Steam flowed around the glass cubicle as she opened her legs and slid her fingers to her vagina. She nudged her exposed clitoris with a fingertip, her mouth open in a large O shape.

Gemma called him closer with a long beckoning forefinger and a lascivious look. He shuffled to the bathroom door, his little erection poking out. He stopped in the doorway. Gemma moved her hips around like a belly dancer. She pushed her finger deeper into her vagina, rubbing her erect bud against the ball of her hand. She gasped as a shot of electricity buzzed from her clitoris to her brain.

Paul's eyes bulged and he leaned forward, almost toppling in his desperation. His hands went to his erection then he pulled them away remembering her instruction. She loved this power to intoxicate her husband with desire, to turn him into a slavering sissy. She wanted him as her pansy princess again.

She rubbed faster, thinking of her adorable husband in pretty sissy girl clothes. She pushed her finger deep inside her, swung her hips and rotated her bottom. Faster she rubbed as she panted and her breath quickened.

Paul watched her, unaware of her thoughts but wishing it was him doing that to her. His little erection twitched hard. She saw how he moved his hand towards it then away, knowing he shouldn't touch it. Learned behaviour from when she and Karlene had turned him into Pansy. Pansy, how she loved that name for him. He would be her Pansy Princess again.

She imagined her husband as a pretty cheerleader with a tiny little pink pleated skirt. He would wear a top with Pansy written on the front and his hair tied in pigtails with a pink ribbon. She gasped and rubbed her vagina. Then she imagined him as a girly ballerina with a pink frilly tutu around his waist. He would be in white tights and light pink ballerina shoes.

Or maybe he would look pretty in a little girl's party frock, pink and flared, too short to cover big navy blue little-girl panties. How cute he would look with white ankle socks with a pink frill and big flat shoes with a large buckle.

Her orgasm rumbled like bubbling lava inside a volcano. Her body tensed as her clitoris expanded into a hard bud about to blossom. The orgasm hit her and shook through her like an explosion in a glass bottle. Waves of pleasure washed over and over and over her. Her body relaxed and her shoulders dropped in relief. Wow, how she wanted her husband as a little pansy sissy again.

She calmed for a minute or two and then stepped out of the shower.

"Pass me the towel, Princess."

Paul shook himself from the visions of the shower scene he had just witnessed. He grabbed the large red towel from its hanger on the wall and passed it to his naked, dripping wife.

Gemma took it from him with a smile. "Thank you, princess sweetie." She massaged her hair, satisfied at the sexual desperation in his face.

Gemma pulled the towel across her back and dragged it across her skin. Her breasts jiggled from side to side as she dried herself. Paul ogled with hopeless desire.

"I have an idea," she said.

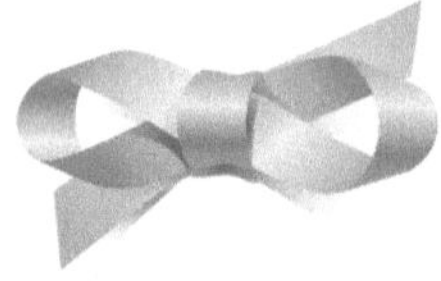

Chapter 3: Desperation

Gemma felt Paul's eyes on her bottom as she bent and rummaged in the wardrobe for her clothes. Her behind was round, firm and luscious, like a ripe fruit. It was the result of the hours in the gym and she'd kept it toned since she was a young aspiring model.

She took a pair of knee-high black leather boots from the shoe stand and put them on the floor. Paul followed her every move with tormented sexual desperation. His flies remained wide open and Gemma smiled at his cute little erection protruding. She creased her face at his sweet adorable little clitty-like dick. She loved her husband and she loved him even more as an adorable little girly princess.

She turned and pushed her feet into the boots, one at a time. She pulled the soft black leather up each leg and it clung to her legs like cling film. Laces ran up the fronts, from foot to top. She wiggled a finger at her gaping husband, his mouth open, his breathing rapid. He blinked twice, as if coming out of a trance and went over to her.

"Be a good fairy-boy and do my laces up," said Gemma, sweetly.

"Are we going to play a sex game?

"Of course," Gemma smiled.

The fight had gone from him and he was transfixed by Gemma's show. He came over and knelt at her feet. His eyes alighted a moment on her vagina. It was open and inviting, smelling of fresh soap and water and of female sex. She stroked his head with a loving caress, her fingers combing through his thick long luxuriant hair. She hugged him tight and let him go.

He shook himself and did up her laces, pulling them tight and tying the ends into a bow at the top of the boot. He stood and backed away.

His eyes floated all over her body. She stood with her knee-high shining black boots shimmering in the light, She was perched naked on two thin four-inch stiletto heels made of shining chrome. She looked down on him, six inches below her eye line. Her slim, toned white calves were encased in long supple black leather to her knees, her smooth white thighs led up to her mound of pleasure. Paul licked his lips.

"Thank you, Princess." She rubbed his cheek with a gentle stroke from her fingertips noting he was not objecting to her calling him sissy names.

His eyes remained fixed on his wife's body and feasted over her vagina and pubis. She turned back to a drawer, bent a little from her waist and took out a white bra and tiny skimpy panties. She put the bra on; it pushed her breasts together and pumped them up. She enjoyed feeling them squeezed together and enjoyed seeing her husband's open lust. A single deep ravine ran between her breasts like a narrow bottomless mountain pass. The tops of two dark areolae peeked above the bra frill.

She bent down again and pulled her panties over the boots one leg at a time. She spotted her husband's eyes gazing longingly on her vagina as it opened as she moved. She twisted her hips as she pulled her panties up and covered her pubic area.

Gemma put a finger to her lips. "Now, what should I put on, Pansy?"

"Why are you getting dressed? Is this not part of the sex game?"

"Yes, Princess, it most certainly is."

He looked at her in awe, excited by her and helpless in the face of her sexuality and her alluring teasing manner. Her taunts flowed over his head, he was taken by her show of sexiness. He wallowed in the sexual energy sparking around his beautiful sensuous wife. He wanted her like nothing else.

Gemma pulled a skin-tight black leather miniskirt from the wardrobe. She undid the zipper which ran up the front of the skirt. She stepped into it and pulled it over her panties and zipped herself up. It wrapped around her rotund bottom like a surgical glove and followed the curve of her bottom. Her buttock cheeks curved like two giant ripe peaches. She took a step towards him and a flash of white panties showed. Her slim toned bare thighs and knees had a light sunlamp tan against the deep black boots and skirt. Her smile radiated like a bright fluorescent.

She chose a white top and pulled it over her head. It fitted snugly against her breasts, following the mountainous curves. Her taut nipples formed two small summits, probing against the cotton.

"Wait for me, Pansy. I want to do my hair and makeup."

She sat at her dressing table, dried her hair with an electric hand dryer and put on her makeup. He watched her slavering, like a pet waiting for its dinner.

She finished, threw him a disdainful glance and got up. Paul's tongue lolled out in desperation; his wife looked every inch the sensual sexy supermodel. Blond waves of hair flicked around her oval face, her deep steel-blue eyes glistened with health and mischief. He drooled over her long leg that finished at his waist height. The tiny tight pencil skirt barely covered her panties.

She rested her weight on one leg, one hand on her hip. Her skirt rose to reveal the bottoms of her tiny white panties and her still swollen labia were outlined against the thin cotton. His eyes bulged with desire and lust. She was like an Amazonian giant against his 5ft 6in of shortness.

Gemma was ready. It was time. She slid his suit jacket away from his shoulders and let it drop to the floor. He was frozen by the situation and his lust for his voluptuous wife. He adored her and he remained passive, allowing her to tease and taunt him.

Gemma put her hand over his bicep. He hadn't returned to the gym and his once large muscle was now flabby, like the rest of him. She pushed close and pressed a bare thigh against his tiny erection and moved from side to side. He gasped at her bare skin against his sensitive erection.

Gemma moved her finger to his shirt buttons. She leaned into his ear, sucked on his lobe and whispered in his ear. "We're going to have some fun now, sissy boy. It's been too long since you were my pansy princess."

His body stiffened an instant then relaxed as she rubbed her soft thigh against his erect penis head, flicking it back and forth. His eyes closed at the ecstasy. He was lost in his craving for sex with his stunning sexy wife. She pressed her lips against his and kissed him passionately. She ran her hands through his long brown hair and wrapped her tongue around his.

She flicked open his shirt buttons and tore it from him. She ran a hand over his chest and pushed her fingers through his brown chest hairs. They curled around her fingers. "A little femboy shouldn't have body hair, she should be smooth and exfoliated." Her words were like smooth ambrosia, enticing and sweet.

She cupped a pectoral muscle and then traced the outline. "Your chest is flabby and weak Pansy," she purred. "Your muscle has turned to flab. The perfect base for a little pair of breasts." She lifted the small amount of fat. "A small slit here and the doctor could push an implant in and hey presto, sissy boobs."

He came out of his sexual stupor. "Gemma, don't be ridiculous."

"*Scush*, sweet princess." She pushed her finger tighter to his lips. He closed his mouth behind it. She ripped open his trousers, letting them fall as a button spun to the floor. Gemma slid downwards, she licked his body as she went down and down. She scratched her long red nails down his body, leaving faint white lines on his dusky skin like tracer bullets on a dark night.

She reached his little erection with her open mouth. She saw the pre-cum on the end, like a small dollop of cream on the end of a tiny fairy cake. She licked it off with a single swipe of her long tongue and swallowed. He mumbled something indistinct. She tucked her thumbs into the waistband of his boxers and pulled them down with one smooth movement. They fell crumpled on top of his trousers. She pulled off his shoes and socks and his trousers and boxers and cast them across the room.

Gemma moved up and inspected his erection; three inches of straining desperation and desire. She kissed the end softly. She raised her hand to his balls and stroked them. Her hand swirled around and around.

"You like me playing with your girly balls, Pansy? I'm going to kiss them because they are so cute."

"Yes," he groaned in pleasure. "Please."

She put her lips to the side of his small balls. She kissed, soft and gentle kisses, small light pecks all over his delicate little sacks. He closed his eyes as she put her hand around his balls.

"Little *Miss Clitty* is adorable. It's small and cute like a real little girl's clitty." Her voice had a husky tone.

She kissed the end of his penis then raised her hand to his balls and stroked them. She moved in, pushed her face into his trouser fly and bit into his balls. She held her teeth there, biting down. His eyes popped open, shock and hurt on his face. He gave a small squeal. She moved back to see two teeth marks dented into his little balls.

"Why did you do that?" he gasped, his face screwed in pain.

She rubbed his balls. "Oh, poor Pansy, did Goddess hurt her pansy's girly balls? Let me kiss them better for you."

She pulled them, hard and fast. He squealed through his nose like a baby piglet. Tears welled in his eyes. She wiped them away with a crooked finger. "There, there, my little girly sissy, don't weep. I will make things better for poor Pansy. I'm going to dress you up now so you look adorable for your Goddess. You'll look so pretty all the handsome big men will want to fuck you."

Paul shook his head, his mouth still tight in the sharp pain from her bite. "Gemma, I don't think that's a great idea. Not after last time."

She slapped him hard across his face, his head swung away. Red fingermarks rose on one cheek. She rubbed his face, soothing the hot mark. She spoke softly. "You're a naughty sissy, teasing your Goddess." She kissed the red weal. "All better now." She stood back, taking his hands in hers. "Now what do you say, Princess?"

He looked back her her blank.

You say, *sorry Goddess* and then you say, *I want to be a well-behaved sissy femboy for you again.*" She smiled sweetly. "Go on, Pansy, say it back to me." She squeezed her hand around his balls.

He gasped. "Yes, sorry Goddess."

She squeezed harder, tighter. "I can squeeze much harder if you don't be a good sissy for Goddess."

"Please yes, don't squeeze them. I want to be your well-behaved sissy femboy again, Goddess. Anything."

Gemma dropped his balls and he blew out a long breath. Her face opened into a wide beautiful smile; her teeth were white and perfect. They glistened and her eyes sparkled.

"I'm so pleased you want to be my Pansy Princess again. And now I'm going to get something for you to make your sissy dreams come true."

She remembered how she learnt how he used to secretly pay for sissy sessions. Well now they were free. In financial terms anyway.

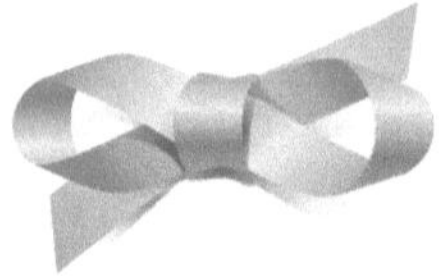

Chapter 4: Sissy Ballerina

Gemma returned to the bedroom. She stopped in the doorway and held up a frilly pink tutu with an attached pink vest. She beamed from ear to ear. "It's a ballerina outfit," her a lilting warm tone. It was as if she genuinely believed she was doing what was best for him.

"So I see." Paul stood with his hands over his erection, knees together.

Gemma strode forward with a pair of light pink ballet shoes hooked in one finger and white tights over the crook of her elbow. "Karlene brought the outfit here for you to wear. That was before I kicked her out so I never got time to put it on you because I got annoyed with her. And then we went back to a sort of vanilla thing." She kissed his lips hard and full and broke away. "Karlene was too bossy with me and tried to take over. I don't want to share you with any other lady. I'm your only lady, isn't that right, Pansy?" she said, a warm loving tone running through her voice. She took his hands and rubbed her thumbs into his palms. "I'm going to make your dreams come true."

Paul shuffled from one foot to the other, caught between wanting to run and wanting sex with his stunning hot wife. Sex that morning with Gemma had been wonderful and it was all he wanted again. Yet he had to endure her teasing first. He loved the sissy thing but it felt odd to do it with his wife.

Gemma inspected the clothes she was carrying. "What shall I put on you first, Pansy-Pickle? The tutu? The pretty white tights?" She thought more and made up her mind. "You need an adorable pair of panties first. To put over that cute little hard clitty of yours. It's so small and pretty I want to eat it up."

"Gemma?" he asked, pondering the eating up comment. "This is just a game between the two of us? Right? There will be no Karlene this time, no big Frank?"

Gemma placed the ballerina items on the bed and picked up a pair of white panties from under the pile. She fondled his balls, tickling lightly underneath. He squirmed and giggled. It didn't take much to distract him. A little tickle on his balls and he was totally malleable.

"Do you like that, Pansy? Goddess tickling your little girly balls?" Her face was soft and happy. "I promise, there will be no Karlene and no Daniel this time." She grinned with a wicked leer. That didn't mean no one else. Just no Karlene and Daniel. She chuckled to herself.

He relaxed, supposing that between the two of them, anything goes. It's what marriage was about: sharing intimate and secret moments.

"There's a good sissy-boy, enjoy my touch on your little sissy balls." She continued tickling for a while then stopped. "Let's get you dressed up like a pretty pansy boy."

She bent down and pulled his hands away from his little erection. For a moment she looked him over. He was short and becoming more rounded now he wasn't training. She didn't want him with muscles, oh no, that was far too masculine. Short and pudgy was cuter. She'd had to stop his gym work.

She lifted his foot and pushed the leg of his panties over it. She repeated it for the other foot. She balanced on the balls of her leather boots, her skirt rode up to reveal her panties. Her camel-toe outline was clear. His eyes shot to it.

She kissed him twice on each cheek. "Tsk tsk, Pansy baby, no looking at my lady bits. Eyes away."

He looked the other way. Gemma pulled the panties up to Paul's knees. The back of her hands rubbed against his legs as she moved them towards his thighs. She grinned again as he shuddered with excitement as she drew the panties towards his erect penis.

"Let's cover this little poppet up, shall we, Pansy?" she said as she tweaked his erection with two fingers.

He shook his head in a trance at her touch. Yes, it was easy to manipulate him simply by playing with his little thing. Gemma tugged the panties over his erection and patted the small protuberance at the front of his panties. She planted a kiss on the end and bit against it gently. "There, all tucked away. Isn't that better to put that silly little thing away, baby?"

Gemma put both hands over Pansy"s bottom cheeks. It was flat, his short legs were skinny and his belly a little flabby. She placed one hand over the front of his panties and glided it around the outline of his small balls.

His eyes rolled and glazed. She had him exactly in the zone where she wanted him. She picked up the vest and tutu combination. He spotted them, reminding him of the situation he was in. He came back from his trance, backed away and shook his head once.

"It's a little girl's ballerina outfit. I don't think that's a good idea, Gemma. Anyway, I thought we were having sex but you're putting clothes on me."

Gemma held the outfit out and admired it. "Don't you want to play, sissy boy? I'm thinking how cute and adorable you will look in this." She thought for a moment. "Maybe we could find a dance teacher to help you to learn ballet moves?"

"I don't want to."

"I know you do, Pansy." Gemma's voice was high and girl-like. "If you want to play then you have to let me dress you up."

Paul avoided her eyes. "I don't know, Gemma."

"It's Goddess, Pansy. Don't forget that." She stared a moment. "Put your arms in the air while I dress you up nice and pretty." Gemma tweaked his erection through his panties and then pulled it. His hands shot into the air in surrender. She scrunched the outfit into a hoop and pulled it over his arms and head. She let it rest on his shoulders for a moment. She put both her hands behind his neck and under his hair which was trapped under the clothing. She scooped his brown hair out and smoothed it flat. She stroked his hair for a while longer, examining him, scrutinising. He had his hair swept back. She pulled it forward, the front of his hair to his eyes in a fringe and pulled the sides over his ears. It was almost to his shoulders.

"You need to grow your hair much longer, Pansy-puff. I can curl the ends. Would you like that?"

Paul bit against his bottom lip and gave a slight shake of his head. He wasn't convinced. He just wanted sex with his wife. If he wanted to play the sissy game, he'd prefer to pay a Mistress. It seemed odd to be doing it with Gemma. Not quite right.

Gemma tapped his cheek playfully. "Don't tell little lies, Pansy, you know you like to look pretty for me." Gemma tugged the outfit down over his chest to his waist. The vest part was low and tight. Gemma pulled out the tutu section, making it even. She looked all around and over him, satisfied. The dress was stiff and stood out from his waist in several layers of starched material, like a frilly pink saucer. It didn't cover his panties, it was more of a wide frill around his waist.

Gemma put her hand to his erection and balls through the panties. "Oh, I say. My adorable little sissy boy is excited by her new outfit." She rolled his small penis in her fingers like a cigarette. She pulled it towards her and let go. She giggled.

Please don't call me sissy boy, Gemma. Or a girl, or Pansy or Petal or Princess. It's demeaning"

"Don't be a silly girl, what else should I call you? You're a sissy." She moved to the bed and took the white tights. She rolled them up and knelt at his feet. She pulled them over one foot and the other, she rubbed one hand up his leg to his knee and back down.

"All these nasty body hairs will need to go. Sissies don't have hairy legs, they have pretty smooth girly legs."

She inched the tights up his thin legs, over his knees to his thighs. She rolled a hand around his floppy thigh muscle. "These legs will look so cute wrapped up in stockings." She moved her hand to his balls. She cupped and caressed them through the thin cotton, kneading them like dough. Paul closed his eyes, he was enjoying the dress up more than he pretended. That was good, she thought, there was so much more to do. So many girly things to dress him in, so many pretty hairstyles to try out on his hair. She corrected herself in her mind: not him, her.

She pulled the stockings up to the top of his thighs. She picked up the ballet shoes and knelt again, putting one soft flat shoe on his foot and then the other. She stood back and admired her work, resting her hands on her broad hips. Her long thin fingers and bright red nails lay over the sides of her black leather miniskirt. Her legs were splayed apart and the hem of her skirt dug into her slim thighs like a cheese wire.

She took his hand and pulled him to her dressing table. She moved the long mirror so he could see. His mouth dropped open as he gaped at his reflection. He saw a short man in a girl's pink ballerina outfit.

"This is only for you, right? It's our private sex game?" His words didn't convey the look of utter pleasure in his eyes.

Gemma rubbed a hand over his erection and swirled it around his panty-covered balls. "I promise there will be no Karlene this time. You're mine to play with, Pansy Princess."

He swallowed hard. "Please don't call me Pansy Princess."

Gemma rubbed his chin, a look of pity in her eyes. "What's wrong with being a pansy princess?"

"I'm not sure it's a good idea after last time, Gemma."

"I told you, you to call me Goddess," she said.

"I'm not sure, I like the Goddess thing either. You're my wife."

Gemma's hand squeezed tight into his balls, pushing them smaller, squeezing his little kernels.

Eeeeeeeeeeeeeek. Paul's screech filled the room, more in shock than complete pain.

Gemma's voice was soft and calm, loving. "I want you to call me Goddess, OK, little girly? It's not much to ask." She smiled and kissed his mouth and cuddled him while maintaining the hand pressure on his balls. She pulled back and stared deeply into his eyes and twisted his balls hard one way and then the other, maintaining a tight compressing hold and a wide sweet smile. "Or I could *really* squeeze these little girly nuggets."

"No don't." His voice was high and loud. "Please, I'll call you Goddess, whatever you ask."

"Good girl."

She released her grip and he gave out a single sniffling sob. Gemma wrapped her arms around him and stroked the back of his head. She pulled him deep into her voluminous bosoms, his mouth squashed against her chest.

"My poor Pansy, would you like Goddess to kiss your *lickle* pansy balls better? Would that be nice?"

His head nodded against her breasts. She had him where she wanted him. Now to turn the screw. "I thought so, baby. Well, that's not going to happen any time soon." Gemma's hand flew to his balls and she slapped them with a flat hand. He doubled over. She pulled him up by his hair until his head was bent back looking up to her. She smiled sweetly. She swiped her flat hand once on his face. He flinched and swallowed hard, fighting back tears. It was in vain as one large teardrop flowed down his cheek.

She pulled his head to her chest and rubbed his head. "My Pansy Girl, did Goddess hurt you? I don't think so. You're such a sissy boy, they were only light taps." She kissed the top of his head. "I'm sorry Pansy-Poppet but Goddess has to punish her baby if she doesn't behave correctly." Gemma's face widened into a large grin as she played with his balls. She pulled his head back into her chest for a deep, loving hug. "Your Goddess is going to make you into the most adorable little pansy boy. Won't that be lovely, baby?"

Chapter 5: Proud Pansy

Gemma spent the next thirty minutes putting lipstick on Paul and making up his eyes. Gemma pulled his thick brown hair back and high. It pulled the skin on his face. She tied his hair into a long ponytail, high on the back of his head. She flicked an elastic scrunch into the hair and stood back, admiring her work. "Who needs Karlene to help me turn my husband into a sissy pansy? I can do it myself."

Paul avoided her looks, staring at the floor, pouting. He would get used to being her princess and enjoy it, she was sure. Maybe. She should have kept him as her pansy princess last time. She had felt sorry for him although she wasn't sure why. Turning him into an adorable little sissy was a gift of love for her husband. He was her sweet girly pansy-boy. She giggled to herself. She wanted to squeeze his little balls hard with love for how he looked. A pansy ballerina. It was perfect.

She took his hand and made him stand up. She placed her hands on his face and pushed his head up. "Shoulders back, chest out and head up. Be proud to be a sissy princess."

Something was missing. He needed a bow in his ponytail. She went to her drawers and searched through them, she was sure there was a bow somewhere from the last time. The Karlene time. She spotted the long pink satin ribbon and grabbed it. She returned to Paul and looped it at the base of his ponytail as he stood placid and still. It was a stiff ribbon and, as she tied it into a large bow, the loops stuck up above his head.

An idea hit her; she'd like to put children's Mickey Mouse ears on his head. She could dress him like a little party girl. So many ideas, so many cute outfits to put him in. The party outfit would be for next time, once she had found something in a children's party shop. Her skin tingled with delight and she felt a rush of electricity in her clitoris. This was turning her on; she'd need that dildo later.

"What do you think, Pansy Petal? Do you like looking like a little girly ballerina?"

He swayed, still avoiding eye contact. "I guess so, if you're happy, it's OK." He stared at the floor. "Are we going to have sex now you've dressed me up?"

"Stop asking for sex, Pansy. It's not nice for a sissy to do that." Gemma looked at him all over. He looked exquisite. The little pink tutu was wonderful, how she'd love to show him off to a new boyfriend. A real hunk of a man with a proper cock, one she could feel inside her. She remembered Daniel: a great body and a massive cock. Not a lot in the brain department. Next time she would find someone with a brain, money and an enormous cock. Next time. She liked the thought of that. There was more to sex than finding a man with a big cock.

Paul had his hands between his thighs. She needed to get him moving, walking like an adorable little girl, admitting he wanted to be a sissy boy. "Pansy-boy. Stand up straight." His body straightened. "I want you to walk to the door and back."

He looked back at her with horror.

He moved to walk. She held him back, an arm across his chest. "I haven't finished explaining, Pansy Petal."

His head dropped, "Sorry."

She puffed up. "Good girl. I want to teach you how to walk across the room, your arms out parallel with the floor and walking like a delicate little ballerina girl. Maybe you need a book on your head to get the right posture." She moved to the side of him and held his arms out with hers, her fingers interlocked into his "Good girl. Follow me and as you walk, I want you to say, *I love being my Goddess's little ballerina*." She moved off taking him forward with her hands. "Let's go, Pansy. Unless you want your little pansy nuggets crushed again."

Paul shook his head but he walked with his wife to the door, hands held out by hers while reciting, "I love being Goddess's little ballerina. I love being Goddess's little ballerina. I love being Goddess's little ballerina." His voice was low and grumpy. He stomped his feet on the floor in the soft flat ballerina shoes. He stopped and looked up at her. "When are we going to have sex, like we did this morning?"

"You need to get this right, Pansy. You're going to have to practise this first. You need to learn to walk like a girl. I want you to be delicate and tender" Gemma huffed a sigh of disappointment. "I'm doing this for you, you know. Now, walk on the balls of your feet like the delicate little girl I know you can be and what Goddess wants you to be. Now again, but this time, recite: *I'm a pretty little sissy boy with a tiny girly clitty.* Off you go. If you get it right, you'll get a treat."

Paul's eyes widened. She saw his mind turning: *does treat mean sex?* He walked guided by her hands, higher on the balls of his feet, his arms out wide, balancing like a ballerina.

He chanted, "*I'm a pretty little sissy boy with a tiny girly clitty and balls. I'm a pretty little sissy boy with a tiny girly clitty and balls.*"

Gemma clapped. "I knew you could do it, Pansy." She kissed his lips fully and put her hand on his erection. She rubbed her thumb on it through the tights. "A good girl gets treats," she said as she continued to stroke his penis through the cotton.

She stroked it and pushed harder. "Little *Missy Clitty* is so hard and cute, Pansy Princess. It's so pretty and so tiny, just like a real little girl's clitty."

Pleasure was written over his face, his eyes drooped with longing and desire.

"Would you like to cum, Princess Pansy?"

"Yes, Goddess, please please."

She stroked his erection harder, a thin smile on her face.

"Would you like to suck a pretty sissy's hard clitty again?"

He snorted in anger. "No. Now can I cum? I'm desperate."

Gemma shook her head. She pulled down his tights to his knees. She tucked his panties under his balls. His penis was free and rock hard.

"Look at little *Miss Clitty*, it's stiff and wants to cum." She pulled his foreskin back hard.

"Owwww, that was too rough," he whined.

She pulled his foreskin back up slowly, then down again. "Tell me you want to suck a pretty sissy's clitty. You want a huge sissy erection in your sissy slutty mouth that makes yours look like a little girl's clitty. Tell me you want to suck it and swallow her cum. Then I will think about allowing you to cum."

He perked up. Her fingers ground faster around his erection. She felt it stiffen a fraction more, he was close to cumming. He raised his bottom and gasped. She stopped. A small dribble came from the end of his erection. He was a microsecond from orgasm.

"Please, Goddess. Finish me off." His eyes teared up, his face screwed.

Gemma wagged a finger in his face. "I want to hear my sissy princess tell me she wants to blow another sissy's clitty and swallow up her sissy juice like a good sissy slut." A wave of electric power swept through her at her words and the thought of what she wanted.

"OK, OK. I want to give a blow job to a sissy. I want to swallow her cum, every drop." His voice raised, his eyes wet. "Now. I want to cum. Please."

"And do you want a pretty sissy to push her hard clitty into your girly vagina hole?" She rubbed her thumb over the end of his penis. A light discharge of pre-cum lubricated the end.

His breathing was fast, his face flushed up from his neck. "Yes, I want that too. Now I need to cum."

She held his little penis between her fingers. "And do you want to watch Goddess with a hot muscled well-hung man again? A sexy man to give me what you can't? I will take his entire giant hard cock in my mouth. My fingers will be wrapped around the base of his giant balls, as my mouth will move along the length of his thick strong manhood?"

Paul froze. "No. I wouldn't like that."

Gemma took her hand away from his erection and wagged a finger in his face. "Yes you would. You're being a naughty little girl and I want you to be a sweet demure little pansy girl, swallowing a lot of sissy cream and having your sissy vagina filled with sissy clitties."

"I want you, Gemma, not a sissy."

"Forget about that, Pansy Princess." Gemma's voice was demure but firm. "You must only now think about sex with sissies. You're not going to be having sex with me again. Remember Lily, you enjoyed her and her big clitty, didn't you? You're not a man, you're my adorable sissy girl now." Gemma stood and put her hands on her hips. "You're not going to be squirting your sissy juice in me, if that's what you think." She pursed her lips. "You're not going to be squirting your sissy juice anywhere ever again. Yuk."

Oh, how she loved that idea. The power to have a husband she could make do anything she wanted filled her mind with so many ideas. Her mind was bursting with the implications. And the fun.

Chapter 6: Gay Sissy

Paul Paige's face was twisted in pent-up desire. Gemma twirled a strand of her blond hair in a finger, round and round, her eyes wide and sexual, her lips full and inviting. She lay back and opened her legs. Her tiny pencil skirt rode up, her panties exposed. She put a finger to her vagina lips.

"I'm going to have to play with myself because you're a gay pansy with a tiny Miss Clitty that has never satisfied a real woman like me. So I will have to do it myself until I find someone who can." She pushed a single long slim forefinger over her panty-covered vagina, a single long red nail pointed down to her sex. Paul tilted towards her and he groped a hand out towards her. She slapped it away. He pulled it back like he'd touched a hot flame.

"I'm imagining a new boyfriend touching me, gay sissy boy. It's our first date and it will be hot. You'll be watching to see how a real man makes love to a real woman with a proper cock and why you're useless." Gemma tilted her head. "Your job will be to clean up his cum after." Gemma slid off the bed, her skirt rode up, her finger poised over the front of her panties. She swayed her hips, her finger dug down between her vagina lips. She closed her eyes as her breathing became shallower and faster. She moved her fingertip faster and swayed her hips, drawing an invisible circle in the air.

Paul jumped off the bed and groped towards her panties again. Without missing a beat, she swiped his hand away with her free hand. He whined like a scolded puppy. She sashayed her hips faster and a light moan escaped from her lips. She licked out her tongue and wiped it around her lips, thinking of her husband emasculated and the large cock of a future lover in her vagina. She closed her eyes and her body jerked. She let out another moan, longer and deeper. Her body shook. Her shoulders slumped and a deep sigh of gratification blew out for seconds from her luscious mouth. Her eyes were still closed and she let the aftershocks of the orgasm ring through her,

Paul moved towards her. She heard his tutu shuffle and opened her eyes. He was on her, one hand grabbed her breast, the other her vagina. She threw a swift knee hard up into his balls. He doubled over and back. A shrill yowl filled the room, *"Yeeeee-owwwwwww."* He flung his hands to his genitals and fell back on the bed. His legs went to his chin and tears formed in his eyes.

Gemma swarmed over him. "Is my Pansy Princess upset?" She rubbed his stomach as if petting a cat. "What's wrong, Pansy Petal?"

Pansy nodded between his sobs, his hands tight over his genitals.

"Pansies shouldn't try to touch their Goddesses, what were you thinking?" Her gentle tone was soothing. She then slapped his face twice, his head twisted one way and then the other with her hand movement. His damp eyes went wide in surprise. She rubbed his cheek and pulled him to his feet and he stood bent over, hands holding his balls.

"Stand up straight like a proud little gay sissy," Gemma said, a smile in her voice, still feeling content from her massive orgasm.

His eyes were teary and a streak of teardrop ran down one cheek. She opened her palms and slapped his face again. She pulled him up by his ponytail and kissed him full on his lips. A faint smile on her face. "Princess Pansy, you know you mustn't grope Goddess." Her voice was measured and calm, as a mother would talk to a favourite child.

"Please stop slapping me. Please?"

Gemma took his head and cuddled him. She rubbed his head. "My poor sweet girly sissy." She kissed him on his forehead. She loved him it was just the realisation of his behaviour in paying professionals for sissy play. That and his inability to satisfy her sexually. This way she would have the best of both worlds: a sissy husband to do what she wanted and a lover to cuckold him with.

She pulled him over her lap, pulled down his panties and smiled at those thoughts. She swung an arm back and whacked his bottom with a massive slap that reverberated around the bedroom. Then she threw another spank. Then again, one-two on each buttock, *one-two, one-two*. "Oh, this is fun," she said and revelled in the act of punishing her husband for his past deeds and for having a small penis.

"Please stop," he sobbed. "I'll do." He let out a deep sob. "Anything." Sob. "Tell me, anything you want."

Gemma looked down on him as he twisted back to see her. She loved her pansy boy and this type of relationship. It fuelled her with an energy she'd never known before. She pushed him off, smiling at the red cheeks. He stumbled and stood facing her. Gemma took his little penis between two fingers. It had gone soft and had shrivelled to a cute two inches. She put two fingers over it and pulled up, then down. Her soft gentle fingers worked at his penis, a sweet gentle expression on her face. She bent and kissed the end with a gentle pucker.

His sobs stopped as he watched her unsure if this was another tease or whether she was going to make him cum this time. His legs were wide apart and his eyes showed he hoped and wished for sex at last.

Gemma ran her hand over his balls, tweaking, pushing, then back to his penis. It went hard and erect to its full three inches. She jerked at it faster and faster.

"Imagine, Pansy. I'm sucking on my boyfriend's ten-inch erection. I have it all in my mouth and down my throat. You watch as I slide my lips up and down, swallowing him, all of him."

He gave a small groan of despair. He wanted to complain about her story, but there were other distractions. She moved one hand to his balls, clasping and caressing them with love. Her other hand rubbed his little foreskin up and down. Her fingertips moved over the little slit on the end of his penis, spiralling around it. She moved close and kissed him with passion as she rubbed his genitals.

She pulled back and stared into his watery eyes. "You're my sissy and I'm going to find you a sissy girlfriend. Think about how you're going to push your mouth over your sissy girlfriend's erection. She has a huge drop of pre-cum on the end. I will make you lick it away and swallow it. You then take her erect clitty in your mouth, Pansy Girl. You're a gay sissy slut so you love the taste of sissy clitty."

He groaned. His penis went harder, an extra fraction of an inch longer for a moment.

"I will turn you around, Pansy. Your sissy girlfriend wants to put her hard clitty into your sissy vagina. She shoves it in. Hard, all the way to the end. She is much bigger than you which isn't difficult."

Time froze for Paul. He squealed in the anticipated release. He imagined a jet of cum shooting from his erection. It would swirl into the air and unfurl like a thin flag of grey gel. Any moment. He groaned and squealed again and closed his eyes. Any instant.

Gemma removed her finger and stroked his little balls. "I love to hear you cry out like an adorable sissy girl. That's because I love and adore you. You know that don't you, baby?" Her hand caressed his balls with a gentle, loving caress. "It's time for bed because Pansy Princesses need their beauty sleep."

"But I was about to cum," he squealed. "I'm on the brink again."

She nodded, "I know, sweetie." She stroked his cheek. "We don't want to have to clear up a nasty mess, do we."

"Yes, we do."

She stroked his balls again with a faint touch. "No. We don't want that at all, Princess." Her voice changed to a hard tone. "Nasty. Yuk."

His face and bottom lip drooped in utter disappointment.

Gemma took his hand and clasped it tight for a second. She smiled and hunched her shoulders. "I love you, my adorable little pansy girl."

He looked to the floor. "Yes, I know. I love you too. But I'd like to cum. It's what loving couples do."

"You know that's not true, sweetie. I love you and you mustn't cum."

They stood gazing into each other's eyes for a long moment. Gemma held his hand and guided him out of the bedroom and onto the landing.

Paul held back. "I thought we were going to bed."

She clasped his hand harder again and gazed into his eyes. "You are, Princess. You're going back to your girly sissy bedroom." She looked up the corridor to the end. The door was open. "You have a pretty pink princess room. Where else would a pansy princess sleep?" Her smile was wide and full.

He stalled. She pulled him along the hall and into the small single bedroom. They stood together, holding hands, looking over the room. Paul was at Gemma's shoulder height. The room was pink and with princess bedclothes. The posters were still on the wall: cartoon pictures of a princess and naked photos of young men, their smooth bodies and cocks shone with oil. A small short pink baby-doll nightie was laid out on the bed.

Gemma pulled his tutu and vest outfit off over his head. She took the bow out of his hair and the elastic band, letting his hair fall over his ears. She pulled the little nightie over his head. He remained sullen and quiet, tired from the events of the evening and from not cumming.

Gemma touched his balls. She bent down and kissed him on the lips, lingering for a while as she stroked around his balls and little penis. A touch of doubt came into her mind. Had she been too tough? She hugged him hard, pulling him to her. He flopped into her body. They cuddled firmly. No, she'd been right. This was what they both wanted.

She pulled back the pink covers and pointed to the bed. He got in with a sluggish gait. She tucked him in and any doubts she had about what she was doing dissipated. She loved her Pansy, but she loved him even more as Pansy Princess. It was how he had to be. No, her approach was correct. She should never doubt herself, she was the Goddess.

She pulled his nightie up. His face lit for a moment. Gemma reached into the drawer next to the bed and took out a pink silicone chastity cage. She clicked it on and grasped the key in her palm. "Just in case, baby. I know what you're like and we don't want nasty sissy mess all over the pretty pink sheets, do we."

His eyes told her he did.

Gemma pulled his nightie down and the sheets to his face. She touched his chin. "Pansy Princess, I want you to be a good, little girl and behave for me. OK?" She kissed the end of his nose. She got up and left the room. She looked back from the hall before shutting the door. "I love you, Pansy Princess."

His forlorn eyes peeked out at her, his fingers grasping the pink covers under his chin.

"Goodnight, Pansy. Get some beauty sleep. You need a bit more work before you're ready and I need some help with that. That part starts tomorrow." She clicked the door shut.

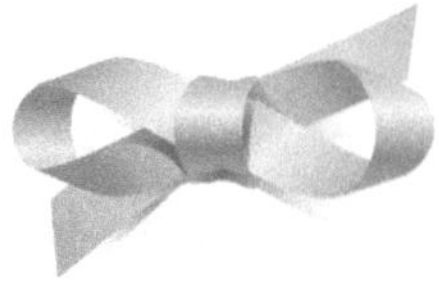

Chapter 7: The Institute

Gemma turned the car off the country lane and into a single-track black tarmac drive. They passed two tall stone pillars on either side of the narrow entrance. Huge mature oak trees shielded the overcast morning sky making the route darker and gloomier. It was like driving through an unlit tunnel.

Paul was on the phone in the passenger seat. He told his assistant Jennifer to rearrange his meetings to another day. There was a short delay. He snapped at Jennifer, "Just do it. Something unexpected came up."

Gemma tapped his knee and lifted her finger to his face. "If you want me to stop the car, Pansy, take down your trousers and spank you by the side of the road, I will do it. So. Be a good girl and speak to Jennifer nicely. It's not her fault I set up this interview at short notice. And besides, as a woman, she's superior to you and you need to learn to be respectful."

Paul put his hand over the microphone and whispered, *"Gemma, it's my assistant on the phone. She'll hear."* His face bloomed red.

Gemma smirked. She glanced at Pansy and back to the road. The car glided at 15mph on the smooth surface. "Call me Goddess, there's a good girl."

"Sorry Goddess," he said, his hand hard over the mouthpiece. He took it away. "Yes, yes, Jennifer, that was Gemma. No, no, I think you misheard, Gemma didn't call me Pansy or a girl. How funny." His eyes flicked towards his wife, annoyance written deep in his creased lines. "Anyway, Jennifer, I'll be back in the office tomorrow. Something urgent and personal has come up. Apologise to the investors for me." He hung up.

The atmosphere in the car was thick with anger. Pansy pulled his coat collar up around his neck despite the warm air blowing from the car's heating. Gemma's gaze flitted for an instant to the tops of his dark blue suit trousers. The lines of a suspender belt and clips against the fine material. Pansy shuffled his bottom and, unable to hide the outline, put his palms over his thighs.

"Why won't you tell me where we're going?" he asked.

"Be patient, Pansy. It's a surprise and you're going to love it." She thought for a moment. "I'm going to enjoy it anyway and that's what matters, isn't it, sweetie."

Paul mumbled to himself as they drove on for another five minutes. The drive opened out and a massive four-storey stone mansion rose in front of them. The flat-fronted building had four large rectangular mock Georgian windows. The building was surrounded by gardens filled with red roses and clipped angular green bushes. Tall bullet-shaped deep green conifer trees lined the drive.

Gemma steered the car up to the front entrance and stopped. A wide stone staircase led up to double wooden doors. At the foot of the stairs, a rectangular white sign supported by two metal poles announced:

THE EPICENE INSTITUTE

BEHAVIOURAL AND COMPORTMENT TRAINING FOR GIRLS

Principal: Dr Fiona Boleyn-Hunter
BA (hons), MA (hons), PhD (hons)

Paul read the sign, then again. "It's a girls' school."

"Yes and no," said Gemma.

"What does that mean? And why are we at a girls' school?"

Paul slumped in the passenger seat, arms folded, his bottom lip protruding. Gemma liked that look.

"I have so much work to do at the office, Gemma." She glared. "Goddess. The investors need an update, I have a paper to go through on an acquisition and our new product launches tomorrow."

She smiled at him, hunched her shoulders and pecked him on the cheek. "It can wait, Pansy-Peewee, this is far more important." Her hand glided to his penis and she grabbed it through his trousers. "This meeting today is important for us as a couple, so be a good sissy for Goddess. OK?"

"OK," he mumbled to the floor.

She turned off the engine and got out. Paul remained in the car, sulking and not understanding what might be more important than his business. He was annoyed at her continued reference to him as a sissy. Despite the secrecy and the oddness of turning up at a girls' school, if his beautiful wife wanted a meeting with someone in a strange school in the countryside he would do it for her. He would do anything for his beautiful wife if truth be told. Anything. He was lucky to have such an attractive and sexy wife especially as he was short and a little out of condition lately.

Gemma walked around the front of the car, her long thin heels crunching against the driveway surface. There was a chill in the air and the sound of birds chirping.

She called out by the passenger door. "Come on, Pansy, out you get, the principal is waiting for us." Her face was bright with a healthy flush in the chilly air. She glanced at her wristwatch. It was loose against her slim wrist, small diamonds circled the small white face.

The sun peeked up above the treeline to the south and a fresh light breeze flicked against her white dress and the small black polka dots flickered like negative snowflakes. She carried a slim black clasp bag tucked under one arm. He got out and shut the door. Gemma bent down, gave him a peck on the lips and pulled his hair forward. She tweaked his cheek and smiled at him.

"Please don't call me Pansy when we're at the meeting today. Please?"

Gemma bent and gave him a peck on the lips. "You are funny, Princess." She ran a finger through his hair. "What else would I call you?" She tweaked his cheek and smiled at him.

Pansy shuffled his feet. "You could call me Paul?"

Gemma laughed. She took his hand and led him up the steps to the front door. She tucked her bag under her armpit and adjusted Paul's hair again. She pulled a lock from under his collar and tidied it. She pressed a small button next to a round speaker labelled *Reception*.

"Why exactly are we here and why won't you tell me? I had to rearrange my whole business day to be here."

The speaker rang with a phone sound.

"No, dear, you didn't rearrange anything, sweetie. Jennifer rearranged your whole business day."

The speaker clicked. "Hello, this is Pixie. How may I help you?"

Paul whispered at Gemma, his eyebrows creased, *"Pixie?"*

"Hello Pixie," said Gemma who appeared not to think the receptionist's name unusual. "It's Gemma Gold to see Dr Boleyn-Hunter. I have an appointment for 10.30." Gemma had used her maiden name, the name she had used in her supermodel job.

"Gold? Why are you using your maiden name?"

Gemma spoke into the microphone. "And I have Pansy Gold here too."

Paul stared at her in disbelief, his brown eyes as wide as plates. The door buzzed, she pulled it open, took his hand and tugged him inside before he could speak.

They were in a wide hall. It was around twenty feet long with a light marble floor. At the end of the hall, a small blond lady sat at a dark wood reception desk. They approached the desk as Gemma's heels echoed against the dark panelled walls. The walls were lined with paintings of rolling countryside and haystacks.

The receptionist looked up. "Hello, Ms Gold," she said with a deeper voice than would be expected from a small slim girl. Pixie looked at Pansy, holding his look for an instant. "Hello, Pansy."

Pansy opened his mouth to object but Pixie spoke over him "Dr Boleyn-Hunter will see you straight away. Top of the stairs, first door on the left." She indicated the direction with a finger and a long shaped pink nail.

A wide staircase with dark wooden bannisters led up to Dr Boleyn-Hunter's office. Pixie flicked her head back, her long straightened blond hair was tied at the back in a large pink bow. She wore large silver hoop earrings and a tight pink top that outlined huge breasts. They were larger than Gemma's and looked unnatural on her small thin body. Her appearance didn't match the stately surroundings of the interior of this school.

Gemma took Paul's hand and led him towards the stairs. She glanced back at Pixie the receptionist. Pixie looked back and her eyes ran over Paul, a hand on her square jaw.

They climbed the stairs to the office. At the top of the stairs, a short landing led to Dr Boleyn-Hunter's office. Her door was open and Gemma saw a dark-haired lady sitting at a large desk. Two plain chairs stood in front of her desk. A black computer screen obscured half her face and lit the other half, reflecting in her glasses. A short thin cane with a hook handle rested against the side of the desk.

Dr Boleyn-Hunter spotted them. She peered from over the top of her wide rectangular black-framed glasses. Her deep mahogany eyes were like dark orbs that shone with intelligence and playfulness. She sat back. Her short charcoal-black jacket was fastened with a single large button beneath breasts that spilled out from an open-necked white blouse. A flash of a deep red bra frill showed; it fought to hold in its straining contents.

She stood and waved for them to come in. When she stood, Gemma was surprised to see Dr Boleyn-Hunter was wearing a tiny pencil skirt, not what a school principal would normally be seen in. Everything was unusual in this weird place. The skirt matched Dr Boleyn-Hunter's jacket and hugged her hips like heat-shrunk cling film. It barely covered her thighs. Pansy's eyes flicked from the principal's breasts to her legs.

Dr Boleyn-Hunter placed her glasses on the desk and walked around and stepped towards Gemma. She was tall and upright with poise, her hips swayed more like a catwalk model than a school principal. She wore her full dark hair pulled back and held tight in a long ponytail and it ran long and straight to the small of her back. She strode an invisible line towards Gemma, like a mix of supermodel, school teacher and seductress in one imposing package.

She put her hand out, a broad smile of greeting on her wide red lips. Gemma was momentarily awed by the imposing physical and psychological presence. Gemma guessed the doctor to be two or three inches taller even than her 5ft 10ins. In her high heels, she towered over little Paul. From the corner of her eye, she saw him follow every step of the principal's legs with a heavy glint of lust in his eyes. She was pleased she'd kept him locked, goodness knows what he'd have done if left alone.

She shook Gemma's hand, their hands entwined one over the other, their eyes locked, steel blue on deep mahogany brown. The two women's hands remained together as they rubbed the backs of each other's hands with a thumb. A spark of electricity shot through the air. After what seemed an eternity, they pulled their hands away. They gazed at each other for a few moments more, an invisible bond linked between them and locked in.

"How do you do, Gemma?" Dr Boleyn-Hunter's throaty voice had the timbre of a British private school education and seemed to vibrate in the floorboards. Her eyes remained locked on Gemma's as if in assessment. Her face softened, announcing that assessment as positive.

Dr Boleyn-Hunter turned to Pansy, her eyebrows raised for a second. "Gosh, you must be Pansy. How divine."

Chapter 8: The Principal

Paul looked like he was about to complain about her calling him Pansy but thought better of it.

Dr Boleyn-Hunter guided Gemma to a chair by her desk, one hand on her back, the other holding her hand. Gemma sat and Dr Boleyn-Hunter pulled the other chair close and sat. She crossed her legs, miles of smooth black stockinged leg hovered an inch from Gemma's legs. They grazed each other's calves, eyes drinking up each other's skin. They looked for several moments more and the atmosphere sparked again.

"Excuse me?" Paul said, breaking the moment. "Where should I sit?"

Dr Boleyn-Hunter took both Gemma's hands. She intertwined her fingers, her mouth opened and she licked her top and bottom lips. "You'll stand there and be quiet, Pansy." She said without taking her eyes from Gemma. Her deep voice resonated around the office. "And be a good girl and close my office door."

He bristled at her words but closed the door. Dr Boleyn-Hunter wasn't watching him, she pulled her seat closer and placed one leg inside Gemma's. Their thighs intertwined and touched, their fingers swirling over each other's hands.

"So you found me through a recommendation from Karlene Adair. How the devil is she?" she said.

Gemma looked away. "We had a falling out."

The Principal waved away her explanation. It was no problem

"Shall I tell you about my husband, Dr Boleyn-Hunter?"

"Dr Boleyn-Hunter is such a mouthful, don't you think? Gemma sweetheart, you can call me Fiona. It's Dr Fiona to my students, of course." Her eyes flicked towards Paul.

Paul returned from closing the door. "Excuse me, but why are we at a girls' school? What's this all about?"

"Be a good girl and stand over in the corner while the ladies talk," said Dr Fiona. "I insist on my students not being quite so loquacious, Pansy."

Paul looked shocked but said nothing.

Fiona turned back to Gemma, moving her mouth to within an inch from her lips. She pouted. "I know your husband from the news. Pansy Paul Paige." She glanced over to him. "He's a well-respected man in the city: a successful businessman. How divine." She looked him up and down. "He's not particularly well-endowed with height or muscles. Good base material for the programme. How divine." She turned back to Gemma, her lips brushed Gemma's cheek. "So, tell me, sexy hot lady. What is the problem with him that he needs to become a good little girl? There has to be a problem, it's why you're here. It's what I deal in: problems with powerful men."

Her mouth was at Gemma's ear, her lips brushed the lobe lightly and she flicked her tongue to her ear. Gemma sighed. One hand rested on Gemma's thigh, above her dress hemline.

"Let me guess," Dr Fiona said. She put a finger to her chin in mock thought. "Would she, perchance, have a tiny cockette? It's a common problem; a powerful wealthy man often equals a small penis. It's an over-compensation reaction, very common." She glanced up at her bookshelf. "It was my thesis for my doctorate. I have it on my shelf, should you ever care to peruse it, darling."

Gemma looked at the bookshelf. It was filled with books, floor to ceiling and the width of the office. Some brightly coloured spines caught her attention among the lines of black and brown textbooks. She squinted her eyes; the coloured books were by an author called *Lady*

Alexa. Gemma remembered Karlene read this author. She guessed it as one of this well-educated, lady's aristocratic friends too.

Gemma closed her eyes. "I love Pansy Paul a lot, but you're right, she has a tiny cockette. It's no good for me, I need more, I can barely feel it when it's inside. So frustrating. He may be rich and successful, but with such a tiny dick I can't stop thinking of him as a little girl. A pansy princess."

Dr Fiona listened with a hand on her cheek, the expression of a doctor evaluating a diagnosis.

Gemma continued. "A few weeks ago, I had sex with a real man, one of Karlene's boyfriends. Karlene and I turned my husband into Pansy Princess. It didn't work out with the boyfriend. Or with Karlene, she was too controlling."

Dr Fiona nodded and allowed a small smirk. "Karlene can be like that."

Gemma breathed in deeply and took a moment. "But Fiona, it was incredible. I tried to return to a vanilla lifestyle, but I couldn't. I want Pansy to be an adorable little sissy girl again, my pretty Pansy Princess. Not just dressed up as a pretty little girl. I also want her trained and to be properly transformed into an adorable sissy."

Paul made one step forward. "I don't think that's a good idea."

Dr Fiona put out a palm towards him. Her lips moved onto Gemma's mouth. She put her lips to Gemma's and she kissed her once. "It's such a common problem, Gemma Sweetheart, and I can help you. Your phone call was serendipity. A student graduated last week and I have an opening for a new student. It's unusual to have any space mid-semester."

She nuzzled Gemma's neck and planted several small kisses around her neck and ear. Gemma shivered with goosebumps.

"My institute is proud to provide a full sissification service for the discerning wife. We have a 100% success rate in turning once-powerful men into gay sissies. Permanently. It's divine."

They both looked to Paul. He cowered in the corner, not believing what he was hearing.

Dr Fiona reached over to her desk and pulled a piece of paper across. "Here are the prices per semester. We are expensive, but we are the best. Success is guaranteed. Paul will become a full-time sissy girl called Pansy."

Gemma glanced at the paper. "That's fine, I'll transfer it from Pansy's account now. The money's not an issue, All I want is for you to permanently transform my husband into a proper little gay sissy-girl." She tapped at her phone for several minutes. "There. Done."

Dr Fiona moved her mouth to Gemma's and they locked lips. She pulled Gemma's head tight and they kissed passionately. The wall holding back their tide of attraction breached and the waves rushed in, filling their sparkling passion. Dr Fiona's hand moved onto Gemma's breast, cupping and moulding it. Her fingers found her nipple through the dress and bra, tweaking with the gentle pincer of her fingers. Their tongues lashed in their mouths.

Dr Fiona pulled back for a moment, breathing fast, her hand moving and stroking Gemma's breast. "I understand your beastly dilemma. You have an otherwise marvellous husband, but you're an incredibly sexual sensuous lady. I can tell you're sadly unfulfilled due to the insignificance of your girly husband's tiny dick. If left to fester, this dissatisfaction and ungratified venereal desire will lead to problems for your mental health. You needed to act, Gemma Sweetheart."

She moved back to mould her lips hard against Gemma's. Her hand flicked from Gemma's breast and onto a thigh. She moved it up and under Gemma's full white dress, the soft material moving with her hand. Gemma whined from the back of her throat as Dr Fiona's hand touched against her vagina labia through the thin panties.

"Excuse me," said Paul. His hands went to his hips.

"*Shhhh.*" Dr Fiona pulled away from Gemma, put a finger to her lips then put it back under the dress to Gemma's vagina.

She pushed her finger between Gemma's vagina lips through the fine cotton panties. Gemma groaned, forgetting that her husband was watching or maybe because. Her lust and desire for this incredible lady snapped and bubbled over.

"Your concupiscence is powerful and should be satiated regularly by strong men with big penises. And by strong women too, naturally," Dr Fiona said, a lop-sided grin on her face.

Their lips and tongues beat against each other as Dr Fiona's hand slipped back inside Gemma's panties and into her vagina. She flicked against Gemma's clitoris and then probed deep inside her. Gemma gasped.

Dr Fiona slid to the floor and onto her knees. She pulled Gemma's panties down to her ankles and parted her legs. She lifted her dress to her stomach. Gemma's trimmed blond pubic hair was a perfect neat triangle and her vagina was open and damp. Two luscious thick labia were wide and expectant like billowing sails. Gemma could smell her own sex, her body fluids were musky and rich.

Dr Fiona moved her head up inside Gemma's inner thigh, her tongue leading against her skin. Paul watched with mounting horror. Dr Fiona reached Gemma's vagina and Gemma lurched in anticipation. The fruity shampoo smell from Dr Fiona's hair wafted up to her sensitive nostrils. Her tongue licked Gemma's clitoris, it was swollen and ripe. Dr Fiona's thumb moved Gemma's labia aside and she sucked on her clitoris. She pushed her tongue against her clitoris again and flayed her sex like a hungry whip.

Gemma couldn't get enough of the waves of sexual energy flowing through her, over her. She pulled Dr Fiona's head harder into her. The waves came faster and faster, her head spun with the delirium of pleasure. No man had ever done it like this. Only Karlene Dr Fiona's tongue was long and soft and seemed to wrap itself around her clitoris. Gemma was about to cum. She felt something special, something different. This was intense. She squeezed her eyes shut. She orgasmed with a jolt and screamed. She screamed again, a high-pitched wail of intense gratification before she slouched back against the chair, exhausted and spent.

Dr Fiona moved away and sat back on her chair. She wiped a delicate hand over Gemma's juices and smeared them around her lips. Dr Fiona pulled down on her miniature skirt and licked her lips, savouring the taste of Gemma. Gemma sat back, legs apart, panties around her ankles, her white dress bundled around her stomach. She opened her eyes.

In the corner, Paul rubbed his dick hard through open flies. His eyes were shut, his breathing heavy.

Dr Fiona's eyes fell on his little erection. "I see your problem, Sweetheart."

Chapter 9: The Office Lesson

"Pansy, stop that right now and put that nasty little thing away." Dr Fiona frowned at him, a face of dark thunder.

Paul's eyes opened as if spring-loaded and his hand stopped moving over the head of his little erection.

Dr Fiona got up and wrapped her hand around the curved end of her cane. Paul froze and shot her an apprehensive glance. She strode towards him like a feline huntress, her tiny skirt creased and tight. His glance fell to the long svelte legs pushing towards him.

She stood over him, looking back at Gemma, whose hair was ruffled, her face languorous. "Gemma sweetheart, this is a perfect opportunity to start Pansy on a trial sissy lesson."

He backed to the wall, his erection poking from his flies. Gemma dragged her hands through her hair in an attempt to tidy it. She shook her head and pulled her panties up and her dress over her legs. She shook her head again, trying to recover from the massive orgasm she had just experienced.

Dr Fiona's shadow fell on Paul. She was twelve inches taller: 6ft 6ins in heels over his 5ft 6ins. "Pay attention, Gemma Sweetheart. You must never let sissies touch their clitties, they need to be locked up otherwise this happens. This is the foundation to make him the perfect, sweet gay princess and a cuckold for you."

She flicked his erection with the end of her cane and grimaced. "Put your hands in the air, Pansy Girl." Her voice was firm, like the schoolmistress she was.

His hands shot up without a thought, his hands curled into fists, beads of sweat on his forehead. His eyes flicked from her cane to his wife as if pleading for help. Gemma smiled at him with a drowsy and content face.

Swoosh, her cane arced through the air and swiped his erection with a crack. He squealed, *"Eeeeeeeeeeeeeeeeeeeeeeeeee,"* and his hands moved to soothe his pained dick. She swiped his hands away with her cane and pointed it to the ceiling. He raised his hands again, eyes wide with alarm.

She walked around him, nodding to herself. "Come over here, Gemma Sweetheart, and I'll show you how we can demonstrate to Pansy who's the boss. And remember, we never want to do anything nasty to our little sissies. We don't want to mark Pansy Princess, at least not permanently. Nor will we ever draw blood. I know you love her. You will beat her for punishment, for correction and for love," she said.

She swung her cane and connected with his little balls. He bent in two and wheezed in, searching for breath.

"Now you try it, Sweetheart," she said.

He looked up, his jaw held tight. Gemma hugged him and planted a full kiss on his lips. He relaxed. She took the cane from Dr Fiona and swiped it at his balls. His head jerked back down again.

"This is such good fun, isn't it, Sweetheart?" Dr Fiona said.

Gemma's blue eyes were wide and sparkling. She breathed a "Yes." She studied her husband. "How are you, Pansy Petal? I hope you're looking forward to spending time here. I want you to enjoy yourself as you learn to become a good little girl."

Before he could answer, Dr Fiona grabbed Paul's ear. She twisted it hard and pulled him upright. Her other hand shot to his balls. She put her hand in his open flies and grabbed and twisted. Paul squealed, unsure which way to turn to alleviate the pain. Dr Fiona pulled hard on his balls. She put a hand to his chest to push away and tugged hard at his little pouches. She pulled up his balls. "Here, Sweetheart, you have a go."

Gemma kissed Paul on the cheek. She then took his balls and yanked them hard and strong.

"And now twist, sweetheart. Not too hard, but enough to know you mean business" said Dr Fiona.

Gemma twisted on his balls and Paul yelped and cried out.

"How do you feel, darling?" said Dr Fiona, sweetly.

"I feel wonderful, Fiona." Gemma's face was alive, a wide grin split her face.

"You can let go now, Sweetheart, and watch this." Dr Fiona stood in front of Paul.

His breathing was shallow and rapid, his eyes wide. Dr Fiona bent him over and aimed a slap to his face, then a second and a third. He back, like a drunk. She followed in and aimed three more rapid spanks, one, two three. He fell to his knees, his head hanging in shame at being slapped like a naughty child.

A knock sounded on the office door and it opened. Pixie put her head in. "Can I get you and Ms Gold a coffee or tea, Dr Fiona?" Pixie's eyes shot to Pansy and back to Dr Fiona with a flicker of interest.

"How remiss of me, Sweetheart. I forgot to offer you coffee or tea."

"That's very nice of you Fiona, coffee please," said Gemma.

Dr Fiona swung a flat hand at Pansy's face again. She connected with a flat sound. A gush of air flew from his mouth. She looked back at Pixie. "Two coffees please, Pixie dear, that would be lovely." She took his ear and twisted it and he yelped. "Milk and sugar, Gemma Sweetheart?"

Gemma bent down to her husband. "Black please, Pixie, no sugar." She stroked the top of Paul's head. "Be a brave little sissy girl for me. This is all for your own good, you know that don't you, Pansy darling?"

Pixie closed the door behind her as Pansy mumbled something through deep breaths. Dr Fiona pulled Paul up by one ear. "Let's take a seat, Gemma Sweetheart, and I'll explain the sissy curriculum."

Dr Fiona pulled Paul to her desk, he was doubled over, a hand over hers on his ear. She stopped as she passed Gemma. She kissed Gemma on the lips. She opened her mouth wide and ate at Gemma's lips, all the while she twisted his ear further. He squealed.

"Shhh, Pansy, I'm kissing your hot sexy wife." She licked her tongue around Gemma's teeth and tongue and broke off leaving Gemma with eyes closed and mouth apart. Dr Fiona pushed Paul to the floor at her feet and laid him flat back. She placed one high-heeled foot on his dick and pushed her foot on it hard. She twisted it in as if stubbing out a cigarette. "Never get your little clitty out in front of me unless I tell you. And never touch it. Ever. It's not yours to play with, it's your lovely wife's."

Gemma sat next to her and followed Dr Fiona's foot movements as they twisted at her husband's little erect cockette. Two knocks on the door sounded and it opened without a reply. Pixie carried a tray in with two cups and saucers and a strong smell of coffee. She placed it on the desk while her eyes flitted down to where Dr Fiona was twisting her foot on Pansy's dick and balls. Pixie's face contorted as if reliving a memory. She left.

Dr Fiona raised her foot and pushed it down on his genitals. She left her foot on him and he sobbed at her feet.

"Where was I, Sweetheart?" she said, lifting a cup to her lips. "Oh yes, the sissy curriculum. You are going to adore what we will be doing to make your sissy husband into the most adorable gay pansy. This is a full-on sissification day programme. Are you ready for that, Gemma Sweetheart?"

Gemma clasped her hands together. "Oh yes. Tell me more." She looked down at her husband on the floor with Fiona's leather shoe over his little penis. She squeezed her hands together. "Pansy-Petal." Gemma's face was alive and her voice carried a hint of excitement. "You're going to become a real pansy princess. I can't wait. I'm so happy for us."

Chapter 10: The Fairy Princess

"Excellent," said Dr Fiona. "The first thing we will do is put sissy on a new diet; Pansy is too slim with no pretty feminine curves. No hips, no breasts. She's not particularly feminine. I imagine she works out a little? Trains in a gym?"

"She used to, Fiona. She likes to keep fit."

"There will be no more exercise with weights or aerobic workouts for Pansy Princess. Instead, we'll put her on a high carbohydrate diet. We're going to fatten her up. Girls have a higher fat content in their bodies. I want her with a larger, more rounded bum and, eventually, breasts."

Pansy protested. "But I'm healthy, low fat."

Dr Fiona looked amused. "Maybe, but it's not an attractive look for a sissy, is it, little girl?" She turned to Gemma. "The sissy diet is about transforming Princess Pansy into an adorable cuddly sissy. We will make her more attractive for other sissies to take." Her voice was deep and flowed like rich molasses. "In Pansy's case, I think cuddly and rounded will be a good look."

"Take me where?" he asked.

She sniffed in frustration. "They will take you in your sissy vagina, Pansy Girl, where do you think?" Dr Fiona's eyes raised to the ceiling for a moment. "Sissy students are required to wear the school uniform. It's a pretty ensemble of a tartan or plaid red mini-skirt, very short, and white blouse, ankle socks with Mary-Jane black shoes. However, we also dress our sissy students in a range of other outfits during class role-plays: bimbo air hostess, cheerleader, little princess girl, Tinkerbell the fairy, ballet dancer, and French maid, for example. It helps to get them accustomed to dressing as sissies. Their skirts are are always extremely short or with skirts with an open front to display their little pretties; we think the exaggerated feminine look helps in their full sissification.

Gemma nodded with enthusiasm. Paul tried to sit up. Dr Fiona pushed him down with her foot. Gemma got down and stroked his head. She shrugged her shoulders affectionately.

"You'll be taking lovers while Pansy Princess is studying to become a good girl. She works, you play. It's a good idea to message her with the details of what you're doing with your hunky boyfriends while Pansy is working. Attach photos or videos of you being intimate with them, such as you sucking on their enormous cocks and having sex with you. Maybe you could take two boyfriends at the same time? A photo or video of you giving one a blow job while the other has his massive cock in your wide-open vagina would be delightful and helps to cement their status."

She considered Paul for a moment. "Let's put her in something girly now so you can see how she will look during her sissification classes."

She picked up her desk phone. Pixie's voice said, "Hello Dr Fiona."

"Be a dearie and bring me in the Tinkerbell fairy outfit, would you." She put the phone handset down.

"Before Pansy starts at the institute, you should prepare her by sending her to work in pretty lingerie under her suit. Ensure that the shape and lines of her bra and stockings show through. That is such fun."

Two loud raps sounded on the door.

"Come," called Dr Fiona.

The door opened and Pixie entered carrying a pile of light pink clothes in one arm. Attached to a top was a large pair of pink fairy wings. In her other hand, she carried a sparkling tiara and a silver-coloured wand. Dr Fiona indicated she leave them on her desk.

"Up you get, Tinkerbell. Which is who you'll be today."

He got up with a deep show of reluctance, his eyes full of horror at the fairy outfit laying on the desk.

"We teach our sissies to become bisexual. Maybe that's not accurate. We make them gay. Pansy will be made to practice giving blowjobs, swallowing cum and getting accustomed to massive cocks in his hindquarters. We get the students to play with each other. We find our sissies love these fairy outfits, it makes them hot. But." She waited a moment. "We never allow them to cum and that's a firm guarantee I can give you. We don't allow sissy cum here at The Epicene Institute."

Gemma nodded, her eyes bright and fixed on every word Dr Fiona spoke. It was if all her dreams and fantasies were coming true.

"To make this work better, Gemma Sweetheart, it's best if you were to strip down to your lingerie. This increases the frustration we want to instil in Pansy. The more frustration she feels, the more pliable she becomes as we transform her into a gay sissy."

Gemma batted her eyes and looked away, a faint blush on her cheeks. She turned her back where her zipper ran the length of her white dress. "Would you be so kind, Fiona?"

Dr Fiona stood too rapidly and, for a moment, lost her poise. She brushed her skirt down as she recovered her balance and composure. "It would be my pleasure, Sweetheart."

She put her slender fingers on the zipper and ran it down Gemma's back to the top of her peach-shaped bottom. She brushed the straps off Gemma's shoulders. Gemma rocked her hips and the dress fell to her ankles. She stepped out of it, picked it up and passed it to Dr Fiona. FIona took it to a coat stand by the door and hung it on a hook.

Fiona and Paul looked at Gemma with identical expressions of lust and desire. Gemma's light silken stockings caught the light, she bent a knee forward. Her small white panties had a wide frill along the top. The sides went up to wide hips. Her matching bra fought against her 36DD breasts, the frill laid against the milky white skin of her generous mounds.

Gemma's smile was broad and her teeth gleamed, framed by deep red wide lips. Her eyes sparkled and glinted as if they were two blue diamonds. She flicked her blond wavy hair from her round face. Paul panted as if he'd just finished a marathon, his face melting at his wife's beauty and his lust

Dr Fiona moved her chair back to give Gemma room. She folded herself into it and crossed her legs. She pulled on the hem of her microskirt. "Now, Sweetheart, you should undress Pansy and put her into her cute little Tinkerbell dress."

Dr Fiona pinched Paul's bottom cheek. Gemma sidled up to Paul and put her arm around his neck. She pulled him close to kiss him. "Oh Pansy darling, you're going to look adorable dressed as Fairy Tinkerbell. I could squeeze you up with love." She unbuttoned his shirt and pulled it off his arms, flinging it across the desk. She stood legs apart. She ran both her hands down his chest to his bra.

She cupped his pectorals and put her lips to his ear. "These flabby chest muscles will soon become girl's breasts, Princess. I can't wait." She kissed him and put a hand to his penis through his trousers.

Paul closed his eyes, his mouth open in desperate lust. He tasted her lips as if they were champagne. Gemma walked her finger down from his bra over his stomach. Her fingernails made tiny indents in his still muscled body. She flicked open the button at the top of his trousers and slid down his zipper. All the time, she nuzzled his neck, her lips light and sensual on his skin. She put her tongue out and licked up behind his ear. He groaned in pleasure.

His trousers fell to the floor. She undid his laces and pulled his plain black male shoes off, then his grey socks. Paul made no fight, transfixed by his wife's hands flowing over his bottom, his hips, his stomach. Light delicate swishes from her fingertips and nails made goosebumps on his body. A small erection poked from the front of his cherry red panties.

Gemma swept her hand inside his panties and he squealed with pleasure, like a little girl receiving a new doll for Christmas. She scratched his small balls with her long nails and moved up and over his erection to the tip. Then down and back to his girly balls. She squeezed them as if she were testing fresh plums in a grocery store.

He wallowed in the sensations of his wife's hands, fingers, nails streaming over his genitals.

Gemma took the end of his little penis between a thumb and finger. She moved his foreskin down as far as she could fold it then pulled it back up, Then down, then up. Her lips brushed his, her tongue flicked over his teeth and she rubbed her her legs rubbed against his thighs. He bent his head up to her; he was on tiptoes trying to recover some height in vain.

He panted like a puppy, his tongue lolling. He made soft girly squeals as Gemma rubbed his little erection. He froze, his body hot, his erection strained to the limit. Gemma pulled her hand away.

His eyes shot open, his face burning red as if sunburnt. "Why did you stop? I'm on the brink."

Gemma ran her fingers over one of his cheeks. "I know, Princess." She smiled, her voice was soothing.

"What?" His head shook one way and the other as if looking for answers. "Please." His eyes watered. He put a hand to his little erection and rubbed. Gemma took it lightly in one hand and moved it away.

Gemma pursed her lips in surprise, then her face broke into a smile. "Princess Pansies don't touch their little girly bits. It's so unfeminine."

His shoulders lurched twice and he gave a huge whine, *"Waaaaaaaaaaaaaaah"*. Tears rolled down his cheeks. He rubbed his nose with the back of his hand. "Please, please. Please let me cum. I'm hurting with desperation."

Gemma moved to him and took his head in her arms. "There, there my poor little girl, Goddess is here for you." She cuddled him and rubbed his head. "Little girls cry, so let it all out, Pansy."

"That's very good, Sweetheart." Dr Fiona nodded with appreciation at Gemma's technique. "Let's get her into the pretty fairy dress."

She passed Gemma the dress. Paul had his head down, his shoulders heaving up and down in deep sobs, snivelling and sniffing. Gemma pulled the dress down over his head and body and smoothed it out. She stood back to admire it as Paul continued to weep softly. He wiped his eyes with the back of his hands.

"Stand up straight, Fairy Tinkerbell, let's see how pretty you look." Dr Fiona prodded him with the end of her cane.

He stood straighter, his sobs falling into whimpers, his eyes were red with tears. Gemma clapped her hands, her face beamed at her husband's new outfit. He wiped his eyes and nose with the palm of his hand. Gemma swiped his hand away and passed him a tissue to wipe his eyes.

His dress was gathered in a powder-pink chiffon. It flared out from his waist. The chest section was tight and his bra was clearly outlined. On the front, **Fairy Tinkerbell** was printed in darker pink letters. Gemma pulled him around. Attached to the back was a pair of lightweight plastic fairy wings.

Paul twisted his head to get a view of the wings. "No. You can't be serious."

"We're deadly serious, Tinkerbell." Dr Fiona said.

Gemma picked up the tiara from the desk. It was a pink Alice band with a silver glittery tiara attached. She slid it into his hair. He pushed his hands up to remove it. Gemma held them with one gentle hand and moved them away.

He stamped a foot. Gemma pushed her hand under the short flared skirt and grabbed his little balls. "Are you going to be a good little girl or will Goddes have to squeeze?"

He looked to the floor.

"Fairy Tinkerbell," said Gemma. "Tell me you're going to be a good little fairy girl." She squeezed his balls a touch harder and he raised himself on tiptoes to alleviate the sensation.

"Yes, yes. I'm going to be a good little fairy girl."

Gemma slid her hand inside his panties and touched his erection lightly. She placed a finger on the end and massaged against it. She poked at the slit and pushed gently against it. "If you're a good adorable girl then I will reward my cute princess. "Are you going to be a fairy for me?"

Paul's moan came from his throat, deep and venous, full of desire and lust. "Yes," he groaned as she curled her finger over the end of his erection. "I'm your fairy."

"Good girl," said Gemma, affection coursing through her voice.

She rubbed hard and swirled her hand inside his panties, pulling and tugging, rubbing and massaging. She told him how pretty he looked, what an adorable girl he was. How the other sissies were going to love having sex with him, Pansy Tinkerbell, the fairy princess. How other sissies would place their huge erections in his little bum hole. How they were going to pull his mouth over their hard clitties until they ejaculated buckets of cum into his throat. And how Pansy would swallow every drop then lick their clitties clean like a good sissy.

Gemma grabbed his penis at the base and pulled and pushed, pulled and pushed. Faster, faster. He panted and gasped. His back stiffened, he squealed out loud. He was on the brink of bursting. He was about to detonate and explode into Gemma's hand moving fast inside his panties. He shrieked with anticipated joy and expectation. The imminent deliverance of the pent-up pressure. His boiler was about to blow. His screwed up face told the story: his juices were on the brink of eruption.

Gemma removed her hands from his panties. She took his face between her hands and kissed him hard and with passion. She broke off, looked him deep in his eyes and hugged him.

Paul's mouth dropped open, sweat beaded on his front temples. His breathing was rapid and desperate. Disbelief replaced promise on his face.

"No," he wailed. "I'm on the brink. One more millisecond, one nanosecond. One more. Please. Please. I want to explode."

She smiled sweetly and tipped her head to one side. She creased her eyes. He fell to his knees. He bawled, "*No.*" His back bent over like a broken arch, his head flopped. The fairy wings flapped slightly as he sobbed in huge gulps of air. Another wail, "*Waaaaaaaaaah.*" and the first sob, from somewhere deep down inside his chest. Gemma ruffled his hair and kissed him again, his mouth was slack but she continued and he kissed back.

Dr Fiona clapped her hands three times. "How splendid, Gemma Sweetheart. I do think you're a natural."

Chapter 11: Big Man

They left him kneeling on the floor, his sobs loud and incessant. Gemma and Dr Fiona sat together. Gemma was still dressed only in her lingerie as Dr Fiona cast admiring glances over her body.

Gemma told Dr Fiona that her Pansy Princess husband had a lovely secretary called Jennifer and executive assistant called Jerome. Jerome was only 25 and pansy was grooming him for bigger things in the company. "The thing is, Fiona, Jerome doesn't look like a typical company executive as he's big and around 6ft 6ins. He has the appearance of a Rugby player more than a businessman He has to duck to get through doorways." She laughed at the memory. "He's such a nice lad though. The thing is, I can always see the outline of Jerome's enormous cock in his trousers. I can't keep my eyes of it. I sometimes fantasise about having sex with this big younger man."

"How incongruous, Sweetheart," responded Dr Fiona. "Pansy is the boss to a real hunk of a man with a huge cock? Pansy is short with a tiny *Miss Clitty* and this Jerome is big and manly with a massive cock. That's funny. If only he knew what a sissy cuckold his boss was."

Gemma laughed. "Yes, if Jerome knew what a little girl his boss was, I don't imagine he'd be quite so ready to jump to his orders."

Dr Fiona whispered in her ear so Paul couldn't hear. "Gemma Sweetheart, Pansy can start here next Monday. In the meantime, why don't we meet Jerome this evening and tell him the truth about his boss. You never know, your fantasy might even come true."

Gemma's eyes widened. Wouldn't that be fun.

. . ✿ . .

"WHY DID YOU WANT TO see me, Mrs Paige?"

Gemma bristled at Jerome using her husband's surname for her. *Mrs Paige?* She bit back the unintended slight but she'd already moved on to being Ms Gold again. She bit back her irritation. "Jerome, you may call me Ms Gold or Ma'am. I don't use my husband's surname any more. I prefer to use my supermodel working surname. Ma'am is fine."

"Of course, Ma'am, I apologise." Jerome's rich baritone voice melded with the background hubbub in the Beaulieu wine bar. They were in the heart of the city centre. Jerome's eyes were large, intelligent and flitted uncomfortably. His face was like a lump of chiselled ebony.

Gemma sat next to Jerome at a small square table. Fiona sat opposite, looking sensational but out of place in this bar frequented by business people. Suited businessmen and women mingled around shiny wooden tables. Amber orbs of light hung from an industrial style ceiling over the tables. Jerome fidgeted on his seat, his eyes shifted from Gemma to Dr Fiona and back.

"Why's Mr Paige not here with us tonight, Ma'am?" He looked around the bar as if expecting his boss to enter at any moment. "Mr Paige is a great boss, a wonderful man. So inspiring and knowledgeable. He's kind to everyone, especially me. I'm learning so much about business." Frank seemed to be speaking to himself. "It was one thing studying for my MBA but quite another seeing the reality of business. I've got so much to learn."

Jerome struggled to keep his eyes from Dr Fiona's low-cut top. She was leaning forward, her arms on the table, her breasts bulging towards him. She had her hair down and had left her sexy schoolmistress look behind at the Institute. Tonight was the sexy seductress look and her black hair waved over her shoulders and breasts like a cascading midnight sea storm.

Gemma looked into Jerome's dark eyes. "Mr Paige is having an early night. He had a big day today so I tucked him into his little bed early."

Jerome rubbed the top of his large smoothly shaved head and his forehead furrowed. He shoved his arm out and looked at a wristwatch. His forehead creased deeper.

"It's 9 o'clock," Dr Fiona pointed out, frustration lined on her face.

"Yes Ma'am," Jerome said. "It just seems a bit early for bed." Even sitting, he loomed like a giant bear inside the cosy bar. His suit was off the peg and showed as it strained against his shoulders.

"My sweetie husband needs his beauty sleep, he had so many new things to take in today. Dr Fiona will be seeing to his training." Gemma took a sip of her white wine "Which is partly why you're here."

Jerome's forehead furrowed again. "Training? But he's an expert." He looked again at Dr Fiona, then his eyes moved down to her chest. Gemma moved her hand to his large knee. He recoiled with a jerk but left her hand there. She slid her hand up and his hard defined giant thigh muscle felt like carved granite against her palm. She squeezed and held it there. He looked back at her, uncomprehending. She saw a spark of something light in the depths of his coal-black eyes.

"You're a big handsome man, Jerome, tall and loaded with muscle." Gemma's hand slid further up his thigh towards the long snake-like outline she could see in the leg. It bulged under the tight cheap trouser material like a giant python. Her eyes flitted on it and then back into his eyes. She licked her top lip. "Your such a big boy." She breathed out ambiguously. One of her fingernails flicked against the end of the outline.

Jerome coughed nervously and put a hand to his mouth. "Thank you, Ma'am." His eyes flashed around the bar and then down to her hand.

Gemma slithered her bottom on the seat closer to him, moving a leg between his. Her red dress skimmed up her thigh over her smooth stockings showing a glimpse of the frilly stocking tops. Gemma pushed her hand up his leg and two fingers rested on the end of the outline of his cock. It was growing. She smiled and sniggered. "You are a very big boy indeed, Jerome."

Frank's face and neck darkened into a deep burgundy shade. He nodded. "Thank you, Ma'am." He fidgeted but didn't push her hand away.

"You see, I have a big problem." Gemma's hand moved over his erect cock outline. She squeezed her fingers over it.

"Yes, Ma'am?" His voice was an octave higher. He scanned the room looking in panic to see if anyone could see Gemma's hand over his cock. No one was looking, but he remained nervous.

"More of a small problem which makes it a big problem. Do you understand me, Jerome?"

His face broke into a shaky rictus grin. "Excuse me, Ma'am."

Gemma's hand moved between his legs and she squeezed his balls. "My husband, your boss, is a sissy with a tiny cock. It's useless to me and I call him Pansy Princess." Gemma shook her hair back as she massaged his balls. "Pansy is adorable, but *she,* be I think of him as a she now, can't satisfy me in bed, Jerome. On account of her tiny dick."

Jerome's eyes were so wide they formed perfect circles.

"So, I need a real man. Do you understand what I'm saying, Jerome?"

He looked shocked. "I'm not sure I do, Ma'am." His eyes flitted to a fascinated Dr Fiona.

Gemma planted a soft kiss on his wide lips. She moved back. "Do you find me attractive, Jerome?"

"You are a beautiful lady, Ma'am. I think you are elegant and pretty. And you dress very well. Didn't you used to be a model Ma'am?"

Gemma laughed. "Yes." She moved closer to him, her hand all over his groin. She kneaded his balls and rubbed at the erect cock outline, her hands everywhere under the table. Her free hand pulled against the back of his head and she pushed his mouth onto her lips. His eyes went wide as she kissed him deeply. Her tongue explored his mouth, his tongue, his teeth, the roof of his mouth, under his tongue, his cheeks. His eyes closed.

Gemma pulled away, panting, her mouth remained open. Jerome was in shock. She ran her fingers along the length of his erect cock outline. "We need some privacy, I want to see this properly."

"Leave that to me to organise, Gemma Sweetheart," said Dr Fiona.

She got up and walked to the bar. She beckoned a young lady in a business suit who had been standing at the side of the bar and said something to her. The young lady nodded and pointed to a door at the end of the bar marked *private*. Dr Fiona returned.

"The manager. I know her. She enrolled her boyfriend at my Institute for Correction Services last year. He's no longer her boyfriend, but he did so well that I gave him a job as the receptionist at my institute. Pixie, do you remember her, Sweetheart?"

Gemma nodded.

"She said you may use the function room. It's the door marked private."

Gemma stood and rearranged her dress. She took Jerome's hand. Hers was like a porcelain doll's hand inside his large black hand. They walked to the door and she opened it.

"I'll wait outside the door, Sweetheart," said Dr Fiona. "Take your time and enjoy his enormous penis."

Gemma found the light switch and flipped it on. The room had a dining table in the middle and a series of dining chairs arranged around it. Double French doors looked onto a walled patio, lit by amber spotlights. A light wind blew the leaves on two potted shrubs. Gemma clicked the door shut and pulled Jerome down to kiss her, then pulled away. Gemma unbuckled Frank's brown leather belt and undid his top button.

"Ma'am?"

"Be quiet Jerome. It's now my turn to give you some lessons. Just do what I tell you. It's your cock I want."

"No Ma'am, yes, Ma'am."

Gemma unzipped his trousers and dragged them to his ankles. He had blue and white striped boxer shorts, his enormous erection bulged inside one leg. Gemma was in a hurry, it had been some time since she'd last had satisfying sex. That had been with Karlene's friend, Daniel and she now wanted to taste a real cock again. She could already sense what the huge steel-like erection would be like in her mouth, her tongue swiping over the bulbous swollen head.

She ripped down his boxers and gasped as his straining erection bounced free in the cool air. Her eyes froze seeing the size. She had never seen anything so big and hard. Cock didn't do it justice as a description, intercontinental ballistic missile would be more accurate.

She pushed him towards one of the dining chairs and he flopped into it, the metal legs bowed. For a tense moment, she thought it might collapse. It bent and stayed firm. Gemma knelt on top of his crumpled underwear and trousers. She put one hand against his giant balls and gasped. One whole ball filled her entire palm; his manhood was incredible. She put her other hand to his other ball and felt them as if testing giant apricots in a grocery store. This was what she needed.

His cock twitched. She grabbed it by the base and skimmed her hand up the length to the end. She ran a finger over the end, circling his wide slit. It seeped dampness. She pulled his foreskin back and pulled her hand back down to the base.

"Is this nice, Jerome?"

He seemed to have been shaken out of a trance. "Er, er, yes, Ma'am. Thank you, Ma'am. Er?" he was transfixed and perplexed at the turn of events.

"What, Jerome?"

"What about Mr Paige?"

"Don't worry about Mr Paige, I told you, he's a little sissy girl called Pansy."

"Yes, Ma'am."

"Good boy." Gemma flicked out a tongue and skimmed the end of his erection. She moved in closer and put her tongue on the underside of his erection where it met his balls. She ran it up the underside to the end then popped her lips on the end and sucked away a small drip of juice.

A deep mumble like a distant thunderstorm echoed in his throat.

Gemma pushed her thick red lips over the end of his erection and closed them around it like a sucker. Her hand was on the base, her mouth around the end. She dropped her teeth on it and felt an unusual power. This huge muscular man was helpless in her mouth, she had the power. She loved that as much as having ten hard inches of Jerome's thick mahogany in her mouth.

She pushed her lips down the length of his hard shaft. She looked up to see his eyes half-open, he was gripping the edge of the chair with both hands. She pulled her mouth back to the end, dragging her teeth along it. Her blond hair lapped against his dark inner thighs and his balls. She went down all the way again, then up, feeling his straining penis skin, his engorged veins. With each downward movement, she took him deeper into her throat. His enormous erection filled her mouth and throat, making her eyes water. She had never had anything so big in her mouth before. And she wanted more,

She pulled away. "Stand up big boy."

He stood meekly. Gemma kneeled up. "Fuck my mouth." She opened wide.

He placed his erection onto her tongue with a gentleness that belied his huge muscular frame. She closed her lips around the end of his cock. She pulled his hips towards her to show him what she wanted. He moved in, his cock touched her throat, then out again, in, out. "Faster," she mumbled through the slab of hard ebony engulfing her mouth.

He pushed faster and faster but with a kind gentleness. His body jerked, once, then again. A fountain of cum burst into her mouth, hitting her tonsils like a rifle bullet. She closed it tighter to keep it in and swallowed. More cum jerked at her tonsils and she swallowed.

His entire body slumped and he was done. She got up and pulled his head to hers. She smiled, large drops of grey viscous gel around her lips, dripping from the corner of her mouth. She pressed her mouth to his and rolled her cum-covered tongue around his. The smell of salty dampness flowed in her nostrils and a taste in her mouth like oily fish. She pulled away again and Jerome swayed as if hit by a heavyweight boxer. He took several deep breaths.

"Pull your trousers up, big boy. We're going back to my place."

His brow creased. "But Mr Paige. He'll dismiss me on the spot if he finds out what happened."

She bent over, took a final suck on his flaccid sticky cock, kissed the end and stood again.

Gemma turned towards the door. "Don't worry, big boy. That's not going to happen."

They made sure their clothes were tidy again. Gemma took him by the hand and back into the bar where Fiona waited with a broad grin. Gemma breathed in slowly. She'd done it, she'd changed her life around and found the life she wanted. She'd enrolled her sweet husband at a school for sissies and she'd found an intelligent gorgeous man with a massive cock as her cuckold lover.

Life was indeed grand.

. . ❧ . .

THE END

I hope you enjoyed this story. You can leave me a review on the site you bought this novela, it really helps me.

.. ❧ ..

Follow me at Amazon by clicking on https://www.amazon.com/stores/Lady-Alexa/author/ B01HWRGJGW
and then clicking on the follow button to get all my latest book news.
Subscribe to my blog charting my real-life FLR and forced feminisation lifestyle with my feminised husband Alice here: www.ladyalexauk.com[1]
You can also subscribe to my newsletter from my blog by clicking on the sidebar and entering your email:
<u>www.ladyalexauk.com</u>
Thank you
Lady Alexa

---

1. *http://www.ladyalexauk.com/*

Don't miss out!

Visit the website below and you can sign up to receive emails whenever Lady Alexa publishes a new book. There's no charge and no obligation.

https://books2read.com/r/B-A-JTBM-TKGJF

BOOKS 2 READ

Connecting independent readers to independent writers.

Did you love *Sissy Husband 3*? Then you should read *SIssy Husband 1*[2] by Lady Alexa!

[3]

Paul Paige has a deep secret from his wife, Gemma. He is a secret sissy femboy who visits professional ladies for a few hours of feminisation.However, he contacts Mistress Karlene who knows him and his sissy desires from when they dated ten years previously. Karlene befriends Gemma and tells her about her husband's femboy side. After first being annoyed, Karlene shows Gemma the benefits of having a femboy husband, not least because of his failures in bed. Paul's future suddenly looks very different.

This novel contains explicit scenes of a sexual nature including forced male to female gender transformation, female domination, humiliation, cuckolding, spanking and feminisation. All characters in this story are

2. https://books2read.com/u/49A5gp

3. https://books2read.com/u/49A5gp

aged 18 and over. Strictly for adults aged 18 and over or the age of maturity in your country.

Read more at https://www.ladyalexauk.com.

Also by Lady Alexa

A Sissy Cuckold Husband
Sissy Husband 3

Becoming Joanne
Becoming Joanne 1
Becoming Joanne 2
Becoming Joanne 3

Femboy Love
Femboy Love 1

Feminized and Pretty
Feminized and Pretty 1
Feminized and Pretty 3
Feminized and Pretty 4

Forced Feminization

Forced Feminization Bundle 1

Lockdown Feminization
Lockdown Feminization 3
Lockdown Feminization 1

Sissy femboy transgender husband
SIssy Husband 1

Sissy Princess
Sissy Princess 2
Sissy Princess 1

Stepmother's Sissy
Stepmother's Sissy
Stepmother's Sissy 2
Stepmother's Sissy 3

Standalone
A Very Dominant Woman
Sissy Pink

Watch for more at https://www.ladyalexauk.com.

About the Author

I am an author and blogger on female led relationships, encouraged feminization and femdom and other erotica.

Read more at https://www.ladyalexauk.com.